7/14
$2.00

EVERY MAN A KING

EVERY MAN A KING

BILL KAUFFMAN

SOHO

Excerpt from *Babbitt* by Sinclair Lewis, copyright 1922 by Harcourt Brace Jovanovich, Inc. renewed 1950 by Sinclair Lewis, reprinted by permission of the publisher; excerpt from *Upstate* by Edmund Wilson. Copyright © 1971 by Edmund Wilson. Reprinted by permission of Farrar, Straus and Giroux, Inc.; "Who Will You Run To" by Diane Warren © 1987 Realsongs Used By Permission of Warner/Chappell Music, Inc. All Rights Reserved; "Every Man a King"—Words and Music by Huey Long and Castro Carazo. Copyright © 1935 by Bourne Co. Copyright renewed. All Rights Reserved. International Copyright Secured. Used by Permission of Bourne Co.

Copyright © 1989 by Bill Kauffman. All rights reserved under International and Pan-American Copyright Conventions. Published in the United States of America by
Soho Press, Inc.
1 Union Square
New York, N.Y. 10003

Library of Congress Cataloging-in-Publication data

Kauffman, Bill

Kauffman, Bill, 1959–
Every man a king / Bill Kauffman.
p.   cm.
ISBN 0-939149-26-5
I. Title.
[PS3561.A815E9 1989]
813'.54—dc19

Design and composition by The Sarabande Press

Manufactured in the United States of America
First Edition

For my parents and grandparents
Kauffman, Garraghan, Stella, Baker
Living and dead
Awaiting reunion

AUTHOR'S NOTE

This is a work of fiction. The places described herein exist in the author's imagination. Any resemblance of the characters to actual persons is coincidental.

Downy beds make drowsy persons, but hard
lodging keeps the eyes open.
—Anne Bradstreet

Practice resurrection
—Wendell Berry

EVERY MAN A KING

1

What he hated most about his Big Burger work experience were the scholarly patrons, every fucking one of them. He hated the Blake-packing girl in the peasant dress who looked past him as she *demanded* her fries. He hated the Marxist history professor, pate surmounted by a copse of screaming red hair, who sneered in regal tenor to his dining partner, "The food here, if you want to even call it food, is perfectly unpalatable." (The Big Burger manager, a decent middle-aged Polack named Stanley, was within earshot.)

He hated the severe "administrator" who dropped her salad—just dropped it, with no provocation—and stood there like Princess Di or some other royal bitch expecting him, John Huey Ketchum, to get on his hands and knees and shovel that shitheap of lettuce and dressing and viscous whatnot into the trash whilst Her Majesty got a new salad, gratis. No apology, no blushing abashment, no nothing.

He had worked at Big Burger at the start of his first semester at college, cooking hamburgers, frying fish filets, and smearing on Thousand Island dressing plus a smidge of ketchup to create that epicurean delight, The Uncommon Burger. Two bucks a shot, of which about two cents eventually reached his wallet. The rest wended its way to his alma mater, the University of Middle York, a bumptiously "selective" private institution rife with maladjusted Science Clubbers, bejeweled daughters of the Long Island Babbittry, weary Manhattan museum habitués who pleaded poverty while suckling on Great Grandmother Robber Baron's trust fund teat, and a pallid procession of Jonathans and Jennifers who got rejected by Harvard, Yale, Princeton, Brown, Columbia, Penn, Dartmouth, even Cornell, so Dad the Dentist packed 'em off to UMY to smoke hashish and ridicule the workaday townies and declaim upon the titanic political issues of the day.

His job—*job*, not career—so affronted his dignity that John Huey quit after four weeks. He had liked his coworkers—aimless city dudes whose beige ID cards bespoke serf status—and had joined in their grousing over the unalloyed racism of UMY's monochrome community, evinced most spectacularly when the leaders of the anemic student body closed the gym to "outsiders," *i.e.*, black boys.

Anyway, his employment in America's booming service sector had ended with a whimper, without so much as an

Employee of the Month mugshot. John Huey related all this to lovely Lassy Dean, which prompted this epiphany: "Hey, John Huey, let's pretend that we're starving astronauts stranded in a space capsule and we can have one last hamburger before the oxygen runs out."

He was introducing Lassy to Stanley, the stolid manager, when a commotion filled the entranceway. There, poised for the humiliation of a social inferior, stood three grim-visaged college boys: camera strung around one neck, *Campus Times* presscard around a second, mineral-studded choker around the third.

Stanley, stiff with diffidence, walked over to meet the visitors.

"I'm Bret Sheldon," said the necklaced one, not bothering to shake Stanley's hand. Bret explained that he represented the Student Senate and had dropped by for a surprise "taste test" in light of student and faculty complaints about the quality of the Big Burger product. The shutterbug brushed by, passed the "Employees Only" barrier, and started taking pictures of the grill and sauce counter.

Next the youthful inspectors, trailed by a solicitous Stanley, made their way over to the Uncommon Burger assembly line.

"Make me one of those," Bret ordered Stanley, pointing to an unappetizing suspended photo of the notorious patty.

Bret's demand had been *too* imperious, taking aback even his compadres, and the Big Burger crowd's collective gaze shifted to Stanley. John Huey expected a rousing rebuff of this peremptory preppie: maybe a right to his jutting jaw, or a justified kneecap to two callow balls, or at least a hearty and manly "Fuck You."

But in that pregnant moment John Huey caught a glint of the most abject hopelessness in Stanley's dull eyes, the resigned recognition of a middle-aged peon, bereft of spirit, lifelessly compliant in the grand charade, accepting of the subject status that inexplicable forces had foisted upon him.

Stanley made that burger, carefully, silently. For one metastatic second John Huey hated Stanley—that servile, cringing, shit-eating Polack. Whither the dignity of the working man, à la his heroic Grandfather Fred, a proud and unstooping *man*, who spoke clearly and simply to kith and kin of the restorative properties embedded in the principles and faith promulgated by Huey Long? Fred had never abased himself, nor had Long, the martyred populist avatar, the paladin of the people, shot dead before he could validate the promise of 1776. As he lay dying fifty years ago, Long's last words were, "God, don't let me die, I have so much to do." Evidently it was still undone. For in Stanley's cowed countenance John Huey saw a universal obsequiousness that he would see many times thereafter as he watched ordinary men and women passively submit to power, to their betters, rendering nugatory the verities he had learned at his Grandpa's knee. The high and mighty, Stanley taught John Huey, did not rule by tyranny so much as by acquiescence.

He sat with Lassy, later that evening, at a university bar with laughable working-class pretensions.

To their left, denimed students threw darts, a pastime that John Huey's landsmen in his provincial upstate New York hometown would consider quaint, frilly, the prim sport of a faggot. At the bar, beefy collegians drank imported beer, spurning the local brew (Genesee) as "piss water." On the jukebox, anthemic rock songs percussed, punctuated by the occasional lonely keen of Hank Williams. No sign of his hometown's favorite, Hank Jr., whose redneck bravado long ago paved over his father's lost highway.

After three beers, Lassy told John Huey that she was leaving for San Francisco the next day to join a boy named Eric and work in the restaurant he had modestly named for himself. "Eric's such a nice guy you'd like him really you would he makes great food and is real close friends with a lot of stars, rock stars and movie stars, which of course is what I'll be some day one or the other."

The news staggered John Huey: not only had he reveled in Lassy's scattershot verve, he had assumed that they would, in the fullness of time, sleep together, Lassy initiating him (for he was as clandestinely naive as most of his lying coevals) into the sexual faith. Her departure, besides leaving John Huey adrift in a world of student council presidents, would rob him of his venereal main chance.

John Huey felt a wrenching lust for Lassy, and only the clamorous ringing of his asshole detector kept him from pawing her tits or making an immediate indecorous avowal of true love.

Lassy was soon drunk, and like an apparition she glided onto the minute, beer-drenched dancefloor. He sat, transfixed, watching her effortless glissade, her untucked men's shirt-tail grazing unsuspecting asses, till she pulled him from his chair, whispering "Let's go home before I fall all over every thing and body" into his ear. They exited arm-in-arm, stumbling and racing back to her walk-up apartment, John Huey burbling "Oh, Lassy, why do you have to go when you've found a complement and a good listener like me?"

He grinned at the brilliant and incandescent fact that the beauteous and effervescent Lassy Dean found John Huey Ketchum—spindly and underdeveloped, mop-topped, squinty (he feared that glasses would veil his clear cerulean eyes), all in all an entirely unprepossessing male specimen—worthy of companionship.

She slammed the door shut behind them and embraced her votary. She placed her open mouth upon his suddenly quivering gape. Her thick tongue thrashed his in glossal roughhouse.

Her limbs were a frenzy of kinetic energy, arms pulling down his pants while her legs shimmied and quickstepped out of hers. She giggled, "I have to go away John Huey I really really do but I want to leave you with something oh please always remember me I think you will." As she firmly guided him onto the couch, a single ray of clarity and insight pierced the boozy fog and set his heart apatter: He didn't know what to do next!

Lassy played with him for a few seconds, hardening his penis to a preternatural tension, while John Huey—frightened witless by all that intricate fleshy hairy machinery—meekly and stupidly rubbed his knuckles against her abdomen. She sensed his bottomless ignorance and unmanly tentativeness, for she maneuvered that thicket of hair till it hovered over his straining penis. *This is it!* he thought, and as a strange and wonderful warmth enveloped him, he felt his cock convulse and its resolve sputter. Through liquored exhalations Lassy moaned, "Oh, John Huey, that's not fair that's just not fair." She dismounted and sighed a heavy sigh fraught with disappointment, his organ shriveling with unseemly celerity. "Damn," she muttered, "I wanted this to be so nice. A nice memory that both of us could take with us to wherever we go."

He rose from the couch, miserable, wishing he could *somehow* propitiate Lassy. Instead he mumbled, "Christ Almighty, if only I didn't drink so much fucking beer tonight. If only I was my normal self."

He said a hasty and feeble, "Good-bye, Lassy, have fun," and heard her say "Oh, John Huey, don't leave yet it's okay you're my friend and always will be" before he closed the door and ran, alcohol splashing in his stomach and adhesive penis sticking to his underpants, all the way home.

Quelled by his truncated midnight encounter with Lassy Dean, John Huey spent the next three-plus years of his secondary education without the pleasurable benefit of conjugal companionship. He was faithful, he bashfully averred when questioned, to his sweet hometown honey.

He left the academy more ignorant than when he had matriculated. The words his grandfather had revered were gibberish here. The simple truths of his boyhood seemed inadequate at the university; the coital mysteries unfathomable.

This, then, was the sum of his university education.

───

After he graduated, John Huey made a brief trip home, to Batavia, a forgotten pinpoint on Western New York maps, an anonymous Thruway exit halfway between Buffalo and Rochester. He journeyed homeward not to see his phantom honey, nor his mother and stepfather, who were ensconced in Floridian retirement, but rather to pay quick homage to his grandfather Fred Ketchum. He found the old man, as he knew he would: alert, devoted, truculent.

As the two Ketchums walked down the gutted, funereal Main Street of Batavia, Fred said to his collegiate grandson, "I hate those bastards."

The bastards to whom he adverted were Councilman Dennis Floss, forever draped in Cornell University windbreakers and ties and visors and polo shirts lest the benighted forget his superior education and erudition; and Mr. Luigi Montello, aged Mafioso-cum-real-estate developer whose raison d'etre had narrowed to one final fantastic dream: to buy the contiguous Ball and Jasper farms out on Route 63 and entice the Buffalo Bills to relocate their football team to those erstwhile pastures.

John Huey thought Councilman Floss more amusing than threatening, the most polished and lapidary jewel of

Batavia's small university class, the lot of whom reminded John Huey of George Babbitt's fatuous, basically harmless aspect:

I've found out it's a mighty nice thing to be able to say you're a B.A. Some client that doesn't know what you are . . . you just ease in something like, 'When I was in college—course I got my B.A. in sociology and all that junk—' Oh, it puts an awful crimp in their style!

Montello, contrariwise, was the quintessence of evil, diluted slightly by the takings of time. The elderly don imagined himself a virile, venerated sports tycoon, owner of the luxurious domed Montello Stadium, an arena in which drugged hireling gladiators who had spent their schoolboy days bullying bespectacled ectomorphs were cheered madly by eighty thousand of their quondam victims every Sunday.

Montello's football fantasy was sheer folly, a will-o'-the-wisp of a man deep into his dotage. Luigi would sit alone in his spacious Main Street office for hours at a time, issuing imaginary injunctions to the pliant Bills' coach. ("You run the friggin' ball too much! Pass, pass, pass, that's the only way you're gonna get somewhere.")

The undefeated Bills of Montello Stadium ("*way* nicer than the Astrodome") would be led by a platoon of slow but game Italian halfbacks. "The desire to succeed," Luigi would lecture the team during halftime, "is the desire to stamp out all obstacles that life and nature have placed in your way. If somebody is in your way, you don't run around 'em, you run them over. That's the measure of desire and the key to true success."

A dozen years earlier, Luigi had extracted the full measure of his community's desire for success. He and the boyish Dennis Floss, impatient with Batavia's crablike crawl into modernity, had secured a sizable federal subsidy for something called "urban renewal"—an improbable subvention for a sleepy hamlet of seventeen thousand souls.

"It will completely modernize Batavia," Luigi assured the City Council on a damp spring night in 1969. The Council's majority was skeptical, but Montello pressed on.

"Let's face facts, gentlemen. Batavia is . . . ah, slow. We have only two factories worth mentioning in our brochures, and thousands of acres of perfectly good land outside city limits are just lying there, not used by the farmers or by anybody. Imagine if those lands were put to productive use: why, we'd grow so fast we'd give Rochester a run for her money.

"And look at downtown. Now, nothing against our fine merchants. They've been very good to the Montello family. But the buildings down there are a hundred or more years old—why, they were standing before my father was in America! They're old, and some of them—I think you gentlemen know which ones I'm speaking of—are eyesores, and I'll tell you gentlemen flatly, because I respect you and I think we're all speaking with honest tongues here, that Batavia will never be more than it is today with an old worn-out downtown. What businessman in his right mind wants to locate in a place where the city doesn't respect itself enough to tear down the old buildings and put up some respectable-looking ones?

"We're living in the past, gentlemen, and the future is passing us by. It's time for what they call 'urban renewal.' It's time for Batavia to move into the future and become the prosperous and very busy city that by all rights it should be."

Montello was no Demosthenes, but his reputation for business acumen exerted powerful suasion. His relentless speechifying, yoked to Dennis Floss's voluminous inventory of studies, charts, and "unimpeachable reports by highly respected government economists" enumerating the case for Batavia's rejuvenation, carried the day. Two years to the week from the delivery of Montello's oratorio of progress, the remorseless destruction of the five-block core of downtown Batavia was begun. In four months, old Batavia was gone.

Fred and John Huey stood now upon the concrete successor to antediluvian Batavia—the nigh-deserted Genesee Valley Mall. Adjacent to the mall was a vast asphalt desert of empty parking spaces, dotted with shopping carts from a chain supermarket. The small businessmen and local producers who inhabited the modest brick edifices of ancient days had vanished with tragic swiftness; Montello and Floss and their allies had decided to attract "big-name, national companies" to New Batavia, and a handful of those giants anchored the mall and the surrounding mercantile district.

"What the hell is this thing?"

Fred pointed to the pride of Batavia's university class: an involuted iron sculpture consisting of two fused rhomboids atop a triangular base, painted a blinding red. The structure occupied thirty square feet of the sidewalk fronting the mall's Pine Street entrance, forcing passersby to walk a loopy detour around it.

The sculpture, which the earnest impresarios of the county arts society had commissioned from an artist in some distant megalopolis, rent Batavia asunder. The college graduates and Men of Responsibility inhabiting Moore Avenue's parvenu houses generally favored "the artist's expression of his feelings toward the mall," while Fred and his comrades, lacking the refined aesthetic sense of the B.A. herd, complained about "that ugly piece of junk."

Debate reached a fever pitch, culminating in an epochal debate on the Batavia *Daily View's* "Pros and Cons" page. The forensic duel pitted Councilman Dennis Floss, B.A. Cornell University, against Mr. Orlon Kern, a self-educated carpenter.

The whole of Mr. Kern's polemic read:

They tell me that the thing in front of the mall is art. They tell me that we should all appreciate it. They tell me that anyone who doesn't appreciate that thing is uneducated.

Well, remember this. Ten years ago they told us that the stores downtown were too old. They told us that if they tore down those stores and put up a big new mall, we'd be rolling in dough.

Well, they were wrong. There was nothing wrong with the old stores. My wife and I used to shop there, and we liked them just fine. It's the mall that's a joke. It's ugly and it's inconvenient and it's a huge waste of the taxpayers' money. You know it is.

So is that thing in front of the mall. For one thing, I can't figure out what it's supposed to be. It looks to me like two poorly made dropleafs glued together and painted by a nitwit. Whatever it is, I don't call that art. I think this artist who made it really took the city for a ride. He pocketed the taxpayers' money and left us with a pile of junk. You young folks, take a look at pictures of the building that used to be where the confounded art thing is today. It was a big bakery called Grant's Bakery. Batavia used to look very pretty, at least to me and my wife and our friends. Now it's ugly. Take a good look at that thing in front of the mall and tell me if you don't agree.

Upon Dennis Floss, B.A. Cornell University, fell the burden of rejoinder:

Mr. Kern raises several points which I can easily rebut.

His remark about our Genesee Valley Mall is a "cheap shot" which means it was probably made in ignorance. Our mall, pride of the hub of Batavia, is outrevenuing the old stores by a ratio of 3:2. That means for every two dollars that we made before the mall went up, now we're making three. I'd call that a "good deal"!

Secondly, the mall is certainly not ugly. Designed by a prestigious architectural firm widely known for its commitment to excellence, the Genesee Valley Mall is quite attractive to the eye, with its clean exterior and interesting geometrical shapes. If Mr. Kern prefers the brick buildings which had almost totally crumbled, well I guess we're all entitled to our "weird" opinions—that's America!

Thirdly and lastly, the modern abstract sculpture at the Pine Street entrance is a real work of art, and we're lucky to have it instead of having to pay to look at it in a museum such as the famous Louvre in Paris. Of course art is in the eye of the beholder, as the wise man said. Or as a beloved "prof" of mine at Cornell University used to say, everyone's aesthetic (definition—sense of beauty) is different. The sculpture is not easy to understand and not everyone has the "tools" to appreciate it. The artist was trying to express himself, just like the *Daily View* has given me the chance to express myself, so thank you and let's all make an "express" trip to the mall!

The debate was adjudged a draw. Floss won Batavia's affluent precincts, but Orlon Kern enjoyed his own fleeting fame. At supermarkets, in hardware stores, on little Wallace Street, neighbors saluted Orlon Kern and thanked him for presenting the public's case against the sculpture and, by extension, the Genesee Valley Mall.

Under a bleak sky, the two Ketchum men stood transfixed before the mysterious rhomboidal sculpture.

"You really like it, don't you, Grandpa?" John Huey enjoyed baiting the old man, good-naturedly teasing out Fred's populist ferocity.

"Why . . . this is a piece of junk, stupid junk, that's all it is. The bastards who run this place have no sense, no sense whatsoever. They ram this junk down our throat."

John Huey laughed at this reassuring evidence of his grandfather's continued cantankerousness, so fierce, so bitter, so adamantine in its independence and its unwavering opposition to privilege and all its conceits.

"I guess Big Lou Montello got revenge for the way the wops used to get treated, huh?"

Fred thought about that for a minute. His grandson had a point. Perhaps the lad was redeemable after all, despite the baleful effects of college, with its smug and suave alien orthodoxies.

The Italians, Fred knew, had long been excluded from the social and political deliberations of Batavia's New England–derived aristocracy. To their credit, the Italians did not beg, nor did they petition: they simply made money, and lots of it.

"The dagos have taken over," was a common local lament, and an accurate one. They built immense gaudy castles, the Nicks and Angelos and Tonys, and they drove white Cadillacs laden with unnecessary accessories, and at Christmastime they tucked wooden Baby Jesuses into neon mangers in magnificently tasteless creche scenes.

Vestiges of pedigreed Batavia could still be found on shady

oak-lined streets, but a stench hovered overhead, the frowzy death odor of a decaying and irrelevant gentry. The dagos, indeed, had taken over. The mall was monument to their ascension; the sculpture a signal that the Third Generation had gone—oh, yes—to college.

All this Fred considered, as a hoary charwoman might remember the various factory owners for whom she had toiled over a long life of labor. Did it matter, really, whether the reins of power were held by a scion of the thin-lipped Livingstons or by a swarthy Montello?

"Yeah, they're all just as bad," decided Fred. "All crooks, all out for number one, me me me me, that's all they know. All of 'em dishonest. They'd cheat you out of your last silver dollar, all of 'em. The hell with 'em, John Huey. The hell with all of 'em. Don't you think?"

"Right, Grandpa," replied John Huey Ketchum, University of Middle York graduate of the Class of '82. "You're right about that."

But the college boy dissembled. He did not know if his grandfather was right. Maybe the old man was full of shit. He no longer knew what he knew. He'd been educated.

2

John Huey left Batavia, and his Grandpa, for Washington, five hundred—it could've been five thousand—miles away. A coveted job awaited him on the staff of Senator Sean O'Rourke, an unreconstructed drunk from New York. The Senator was a favorite of the press corps, whom he dazzled with misspoken Keats quotes and half-assed Brendan Behan allusions, all the while tanked to his ruddybloody gills with Scotch.

O'Rourke was a rare breed: a dipso who doubled as martinet. He was never so drunk that he couldn't abuse a minion. Just when a staffer thought that inebriation might save him from a tongue-lashing for some peccadillo or other, Senator Sean roused himself out of bleary stupor, wiped the omniflowing snot from his bulbous nose, and bellowed, "Jesus Bloody Fucking Christ! Is my own staff against me? Have you all joined in league against me? If I wasn't a gentleman, I'd wring your bloody fucking neck. Take your leave, sir!"

At which point the upbraided staffer would slink from O'Rourke's sanctum, cursing his luck and wondering how a shanty Irishman had acquired a profane Episcopalian vocabulary.

John Huey seldom saw O'Rourke, to his great relief. His job was Legislative Correspondent, which entailed writing anodyne responses to anguished, angry, anxious, or lunatic constituents. A daunting and very impressive charge, thought a corps of twenty-two-year-old O'Rourkians, and John Huey would spend hours agonizing over verb selection and apposite quotes for his letters. (The Senator insisted that his ghostwriters, too, feign erudition.)

In John Huey's second month on the job, Bertram Moost joined the O'Rourke office. They were given adjacent desks in LegCor hell, an anteroom far from command central. Grousing over their lack of importance in the Senate universe forged the initial bond between the two friends; complaints begat cynical jokes begat drinking bouts begat friendship.

Who was Bertram? A jowly fellow with pale, almost marmoreal skin. He was plump, fat really, but he never sought to camouflage his bulk with baggy clothes. He wore exquisitely tailored suits that highlighted every dewlap, and he often planted a red hanky in his left pocket.

He was only twenty-four when John Huey met him, yet Bertram's dress suggested a foppish Victorian. He was seldom without a bowler atop his head, cocked a shade to the right because, he avowed, "Albert Jay Nock wore it just so. As Nock's heir by acclamation, I ought to genuflect to the old boy now and then, don't you think?"

His vanity was so transparent, so obviously affected, that no one thought him a jerk. And the lilt in Bertram's voice so entranced his mates that none dared tell him that Nock would regard his descendant as a fat pig whose dandified airs transliterated into lifeless, artless prose.

Occasionally Bertram carried a cane. He did so ostentatiously, for he loved people to question him about it.

PARTY-GOER: Why do you walk with a cane? Did you hurt your leg?

BERTRAM: No, no, my good man. It's an affectation.

He'd stolen the joke, but the trivial plagiarism went unfootnoted with every repetition.

Though his girth gave him an asexual, physically amorphous presence, Bertram was a hit at young conservatives' parties. These affairs were decidedly unfestive, most gatherings fissioning into ten or twelve cells of earnest and dull activists regurgitating the slop that their publicist heroes had written during the past week.

Bertram would stand, a blimpish statue, about a foot from the hors d'oeuvres table. He felt no palpable shame or embarrassment at grabbing two, five, ten shrimp or clumps of soft cheese and popping them into his circular maw, swallowing anything smaller than a grapefruit whole. When he needed to belch he did so, loudly, into his red hanky, with such aplomb that no one thought him an oaf. He just stood there, a cross between G. K. Chesterton and Mr. Peanut, devouring the yuppie food, burping, and lecturing rightwing coeds on Russell Kirk's notion of virtue.

John Huey hit these parties with some regularity in his earliest Washington days. He'd tell the host, "Yeah, maybe I'll come, I'll try to be there," when invited. Then he'd spend the twenty-four hours preceding the party lost in erotic reverie, always meeting a slight, four-eyed, brainy girl who sat alone in the corner reading William Dean Howells. She'd shyly accept John Huey's invitation to dance, do so with engaging clumsiness, then they'd walk off into the crisp Potomac night, an evening of unspoken sexual pleasure awaiting them. The girl's name was Kara, and in her lithe arms John Huey frolicked in salacious preparty fantasy. Spent from Kara's gentle ministrations, John Huey was ready to gather with the conservative bacchants.

He'd slip into the party unnoticed and seek out Bertram at the chow table.

"Ah, Dr. Ketchum," Bertram would exclaim as John Huey approached. "So good of you to set aside your monograph on Ortega y Gasset to revel with us."

John Huey vaguely knew who Ortega y Gasset was, and he knew damn well that Bertram hadn't digested *Revolt of the Masses*. But it was an old gag, spoken in their secret language of friends, and besides, thought John Huey, it puzzled the hell out of twenty-one-year-old interns from Bob Jones University.

The year and a half in O'Rourke's employ instilled an overriding skepticism in John Huey, a suspicion that all great men are impostors, bombastic Wizards of Oz whose staff-directed sound and fury are magnificent displays of fraudulence and flatulence, operatically staged and brilliantly deceptive. The American myth makers, he concluded, were right: Anyone can be president. A shit-faced, atrabilious Senator served as Exhibit A.

The Capitol Hill staffers he met (Bertram and a handful of others excluded) were purgatory-bound political drones, laboring in barren orchards, stomping people into grapeshot. Their walks were purposeful, their voices urgent, their silences fraught with meaning as they hustled in packs up and down the echoing corridors of the great Washington formicary of Constitution Avenue.

One Sunday night, recuperating from a carousal the night before, John Huey and Bertram faced a pile of pleading, argumentative, adulatory, bleeding letters from a thousand dread *constituents*. (The whole office pronounced the word with dripping disdain.) The duo had been drinking (two six-packs of Heineken purloined from the Senator's hidden refrigerator) and were in no mood, or shape, to draft lucid replies.

So they sifted through the stack, removing the ten or twelve most pathetic samples. "My Dear Senato OR'ork," began one, "I write you to know that my brother Carlos can't relat a job but he try so hard so, I think you can help Carlos." It went on, four barely decipherable paragraphs of Puerto Rican patois, a pitiable request for aid to a Great

Man as distant from the barrio as Jesus Fucking Christ himself.

"Methinks the señorita is muy forlorn," declared Bertram, prevenient to a resounding belch. "So let us succor the supplicating señorita." He skipped, staccatoish, over the alliteration, spittle spraying from his mouth.

"Muy pussy!" shouted John Huey, head swimming in booze. "I want the señorita's hot little slut pussy." A vain boast—alcohol had ensured that.

"Hark, good fellow," bellowed Bertram, "an idea approaches." He shut his eyes to hasten its arrival. He called John Huey over to his word processor and revealed his brainchild. Five minutes of helter-skelter keyboard-pecking later, a letter to Miss Rosie Velez was typed out on the NLQ printer, on U.S. Senate stationery.

DEAR MISS VELEZ:

I have received your letter intended for Senator O'Rourke. Rather than pass it on to his fatigued form, I am taking the liberty of replying to you myself.

Fuck Carlos. He's a loser. Get him a paper route or something. No?

As for you, I want to taste your creamy little Spanish dribblings on my tongue. I'm hot for you, Rosie, real hot. I'd abdicate my Senate throne for one kiss from your Latin mouth. If our first date goes well, perhaps we'll have a second. We'll tussle in the back seat of my limo, and I shan't observe one single Senatorial courtesy.

Do you read me, Rosie? I'm enclosing a photo. Imagine

a 10-inch legislative staff bulging in those trousers and you'll get the full picture.

Please write back. I can't live without you.

SINCERELY,

Senator John Herndt

Herndt was a Pennsylvania Republican with "plenty of noblesse oblige," said Bertram, "as long as the subjects know who's monarch and who's liege."

Bertram signed Herndt's name to the letter, a competent forgery, and as he crossed the "t" with a flourish the conspirators erupted in beery laughter.

John Huey, who'd composed the bulk of the epistle, doubled over, gasping for breath and saying "ohnoohnoohno," till a drop squeezed out his eye. Bertram's laugh was heartier, jovial, dignified, and framed a brief belching fit.

The forgers began a second letter, from Herndt to an elderly woman whose chickenscratch deplored animal experimentation ("they have souls, too, Senator"), but the Heinekens had sapped their mischievous energy.

So they made one last foray into O'Rourke's armamentarium, selecting an untouched pint of Johnny Walker and filling two shot glasses to the brim, splashing the overflow on O'Rourke's carpet. They toasted. "To the people of New York!" declaimed John Huey, "who in their boundless wisdom have sent an infirm monkey-spanking drunk to the ghost chamber."

Giggling and staggering, the duo returned to their work enclave. There sat an immense pile of letters.

"The solution is obvious, my good fellow." Bertram was swaying in his rotund way, not unlike an elongated buoy bobbing in the water. "Ashes to ashes, dust to dust, papyrus to. . . ." he halted, scavenging his brain for a sensible destination. Drink had rendered him incoherent.

"Only one thing to do, man," said a suddenly energetic John Huey. "Toss this shit."

"Yes!" Bertram pounded his desk with open palms.

"To the bins, man, to the bins."

They dumped the democratic communications of the anonymous manswarm into three knee-high wastebaskets, which they carried—furtively, secretly, though not a soul was in sight—to the industrial dumpsters in the basement of the Russell Senate Office Building.

Bertram held one basket poised on the brink of evacuation above the dumpster. With his free hand he blessed himself, sacerdotally grave. He administered extreme unction to the basket—"Res Publica, rest in peace"—and emptied its contents. They hit bottom with an impressive thud.

The other two baskets were similarly blessed and disposed of. After which the drunken public servants went home, and the commonweal slept.

Their welcomes worn out, John Huey and Bertram Moost then jumped ship together, soon landing in the turbid waters of one of those Washington foundations that are known as think tanks.

On the basis of their experience at the exalted Senatorial

level they were signed on by the PR team at the opulently endowed and appointed American Foundation, a free-spending conservative think tank nourished by the limitless cash infusions of a handful of elderly Republican Medicis. Like so many other panegyrists of the free market, the Foundation claimed charitable tax-exempt status (501(c)(3)), thus shielding itself from the bracing winds of the venerated God Competition. But that's another story.

John Huey last saw his beloved grandfather in the interregnum between jobs. Fred, when apprised of his grandson's prospective change of employer, hadn't a clue what the American Foundation was, and John Huey wasn't about to tell him that he was going on the payroll of a tight-assed, Pinkerton-souled brainiary, an institution that oozed anti-Huey Longism, from its Scholars Dining Room to the oleaginous handshakes of the bespectacled, mephitic-breathed AF fund-raising team.

He sometimes wondered how the money-raisers would treat Fred if he showed up one day, a convert to the rightist cause. Would they pump his hand, smearing foul power-lunch sweat into the leathern, craggy ridges between his fingers? Would they introduce him to an American Foundation Fellow or two, secretly smirking at the intellectual canyon they wrongly assumed separated the salaried thinker from the hick? If they smelled a $5,000-plus donation, they'd doubtless take Fred to lunch at the nearby Monocle, casually acknowledging the nods of illuminati co-conspirators and whispering, in words cumbrous with self-importance, banal sentence fragments about Washington arcana: "The continuing resolution may not fly. . . . Things are crazy here today, but in this town they always are. . . . Congress is working its ass off, but who can tell what's on Budget's mind. . . . It's a zoo. A wild, wild town."

For $10,000 Fred would get lunch with a distracted, frequently drunk right-wing senator.

Of course if Fred hadn't money, or the appearance thereof, he'd get a brochure and a chaperoned walk out the exit door.

John Huey still loved his Grandpa but found his view of the world . . . *limited*. The simplistic, Manichean dualities of Huey Long—rural good, urban bad; work and farm good, finance and large-scale industry bad; voiceless people good, Rockefellers and Mellons and Baruchs and Carnegies and Roosevelts bad—he'd long ago dismissed as provincial sentimentality. And Fred's natural, fluent idiom of class resentment and chauvinism John Huey had chalked up to ignorance. He disliked retracing the thought process that led him to embrace much of the American Foundation creed, but it seemed to him, then, an inevitable evolution—the honing and disciplining of a mind previously given to superstition and regionalist bias. He'd simply grown up.

On his final visit he had found Fred inspirited as ever by the sight of his descendant, even one as wretchedly traitorous as John Huey. Fred asked him to take a drive along their usual sinuous route, past the onion fields and rundown barns and impossibly shallow streams that led nowhere. As John Huey drove, Fred settled back in the passenger seat and wandered down his favorite path of inquiry, for the last time.

"This is beautiful, isn't it John Huey?" he asked as they drove into the great blue maw of the open sky.

"Sure is, Grandpa." *Please don't ask what you're going to ask.*

"Wouldn't you like to live here again?"

He'd known Fred was going to ask.

"Uh, yeah, maybe someday." John Huey thought of turning on the car radio, decided against it.

"Well, why not today? Why someday?"

"Well, there's just no job opportunities here, Grandpa," he said. "I couldn't do the things I'm doing now if I lived in Batavia. There's just no market for it."

"Like what things?" Fred was always puzzled by his grandson's DC employment. "What *do* you do, John Huey?"

"Work. At the Senate until now. I start in a couple weeks at the American Foundation." John Huey saw no need to explain the reason for his change of employers. And he felt silly discussing these remote, ethereal mind factories, so distant from a one-lane Genesee County back road.

But Fred persisted. "What are you going to do at this Foundation?"

"Public relations stuff, you know, writing press releases and all that." (*Indispensable stuff, yup.*)

"Why can't you do that in Batavia?"

"You just can't. All the action is in the big cities." John Huey was impatient at yet another performance of the

"Come-Home—I-Can't" minidrama. He liked the characters, but the plot was overfamiliar.

"Oh, okay. Maybe someday," Fred said, signaling that act's end. They moved onto other subjects, politics included. John Huey never divulged the nature of the American Foundation's program, and Fred never asked. Fred might have suspected the boy's recusancy; John Huey had no idea if the old man was disappointed by his only heir's divergence from Long principles.

The rest of the ride went like the thousands before it. They drove all through the lonely Western New York countryside, Fred expounding upon the President ("that jerk"), local politicians ("all in it for the money, gimmegimmegimme, the money and the power, bah"), and the crimes and pretenses of Batavia's plutocracy ("goddam jerks think they're better than the people; they're no better than anyone else"). They sped the final mile or two, for John Huey was staying with a friend in Buffalo and wanted to get there in plenty of time for a bibulous evening.

"Bye, Grandpa," he said as he hopped into his buddy's car. "See you soon." Three weeks later Fred was dead. Old age—that implacable bastard—killed him.

3

The American Foundation, resplendent in sparkling marble, occupied an entire block of Washington's Capitol Hill district.

Its four sprawling stories, if rendered topographically, would resemble a polychromatic layer cake. The base was black, basic black, color of the switchboard operators and liveried janitors and sullen mail clerks whose meager paychecks constituted the tiniest slice of the annual budget pie.

The second layer, light brown in hue, was known informally as Tijuana North. This floor was reserved for emissaries of the Foundation's kindred foreign spirits. Here contemplated Mexican free-market economists, Latin American caudillos-in-exile, Moslems intent on Westernizing their superstitious brethren, and Africans eager to depose that forsaken continent's numberless anti-American dictators and install newly minted pro-American tyrants. Most of these second-floor outliers stayed for a year at most, producing one or two unreadable "issue papers" and nicely mottling the composite complexion of the Foundation's frequent symposia.

The third floor, christened the Brain Trust by its residents, was devoted to the formulation and propagation of the conservative faith—as defined by the Foundation's directorate. In vain might the curious visitor search for evidence of the Mugwump conservatism of Henry Adams, the gallant localist conservatism of Jefferson Davis, the rumbustious anarchist conservatism of John dos Passos, or any of a thousand brilliant and singular mutations. The American Foundation, its patrons and clients (including the scurrying ants of 1600 Pennsylvania Avenue) in lockstep, held to a peculiar and astringent doctrine admixing unstinting loyalty to big business with a perfervid enthusiasm for all things military. The resulting alloy they called "conservatism," and on its behalf they sacrificed forests of paper and covens of smiling senior fellows, all to quench the unquenchable appetite of the Goddess Media.

The denizens of the Brain Trust, the floormates of John Huey Ketchum and Bertram Moost, prided themselves on impetuosity and the devil-may-care flair of the engaged intellectual, within limits, of course. To proclaim their bohemianism, many wore shocking-yellow or Hendrix-purple ties, making Floor Three a white quilt with blinding swatches of rainbow color.

The brain trusters also cursed blue streaks when they felt like it, and if the boss was beyond earshot they imprecated him freely, befouling the air with vainglorious threats to "fuck him in the ass," "hang him by the balls," or "defenestrate the cocksucker."

When, however, in the presence of any of the dozen sober-sided vice presidents and potentates of Floor Four, the brain trusters whimpered and purred and became erect when petted. They whimpered, "Good morning, Mr. Troy." They whimpered, "That was an excellent piece you wrote for *Human Events*, Miss Bishop." They whimpered, "I'd be flattered if you'd read my essay and offer any comments, Mr. Gately."

The Troys and Bishops and Gatelys before whom the brain trusters groveled were the pale white demiurges of the clouds, Floor Four, an impervious club whose middle-aged members had met in the watershed Goldwater campaign of 1964, flush with chiliastic zeal. The intervening years had seen that zeal congeal and then slowly putrefy into a conventional careerist mold.

"Well, we've grown up, that's for sure, and we have a realistic view of the way the world works," is how the cloud people explained their evolution. "The American Foundation is now a permanent part of the political landscape," they were also fond of saying, and in fixity, apparently, begins responsibility.

The American Foundation, like any hierarchy, was not a fun place to work. So its superterranean employees consoled themselves with too-eager avowals that they operated in the eye of a great gathering ideological storm. As the Foundation's director of defense policy—a scrawny Vietnam-era 4-F, withal—once said in the borrowed argot of the hip: "This is where it all comes down, baby. This is where the you-know-what hits the fan. This is where Uncle Sam gets its marching orders to kick rear end and take names."

Or as Bertram was fond of telling John Huey, "We are the alchemists of the post-Enlightenment, my good man. We gild the dross of politics and watch as the Fourth Estate marvels at the gleaming golden nuggets."

Great pains were taken at the American Foundation and at opposing think tanks to impress upon the world the irreconcilable natures of the two competing public philosophies that undergirded modern American politics. Foundation analysts and their opposite numbers excoriated each other in print and on television, issuing dark, portentous warnings of the dire fate that awaited Americans if the combatants' adversaries attained political power. In summer, softball games were played between rival think tanks, and the games were fierce.

So it surprised any number of observers when American Foundation Vice President Morris Hackett announced that the speaker at the Foundation's annual Theodore Roosevelt Memorial Lecture was to be none other than Senator Sean

O'Rourke, stalwart Democrat and knightly foe of all Foundation works.

"Ah, splendid," rejoiced Bertram at the news. "Our paragon comes a-calling, fortified by grog, to commend his erstwhile aides-de-camp for their service to the republic. We shall both be quite moved, I hazard to say."

"Yeah, right," replied his fellow ex-O'Rourkian. "Look, Bert, don't you see? We're fucked. What happens when that asshole O'Rourke finishes his speech and makes a beeline to the bar? Some jerk-off colleague of ours is gonna corner the old drunk and tell him how his former top aides Ketchum and Moost are here, and wouldn't he like to say hi to them and reminisce about old times? Even in lucid moments he probably wouldn't remember us, and if he's cocked—and you know he will be—he's liable to say 'Who the hell are they?' and then we'll be so damn humiliated we'll have to bow our heads in shame and start hanging out on the First Floor. We'll be fucking déclassé."

Bertram swallowed a cupcake and pondered their fix. When he spoke, ejecta of saliva carried unmasticated cupcake particles to a shag resting place.

"I see your point, fellow. We may have prevaricated a tad. Fear not, I'll apply my charms to Miss Doris Evans (the Senator's personal secretary), and she shall remind the statesman of our manifold contributions to the polity. Fear not, fear not, fear not."

With that incantation Bertram set forth for the vending machines and the crisis passed.

Senator Sean O'Rourke swayed behind the podium, the slow oscillation of his trunk giving him a strangely lissome appearance. He ran his left hand through his thick black hair, rubbing his forehead as if to restore order inside, and he began the Theodore Roosevelt Memorial Lecture.

"My friends," he harrumphed, "friends and foes and friends again, I come in peace." At this point the speechwriter had inserted between parentheses, ". . . and hope to leave in one piece," but O'Rourke thought the joke unfunny and beneath the dignity of a United States Senator, so he skipped it.

John Huey rolled his eyes when presently O'Rourke fumbled the word "faction," for he knew that this presaged several hackneyed paragraphs misinterpreting James Madison and dragooning that old French fool de Tocqueville into the speech. John Huey had recently come across a wonderful letter written by Thomas Hart Benton to Martin Van Buren in which Old Bullion snapped, "Have you read Tocqueville? He is the authority in Europe and with the federalists here and will be with our posterity if they know nothing but what the federalists write." Benton had reason to grieve: a century and a half later, Alexis was quoted with equal ardor by ghostwriters on both sides of the American political divide, and John Huey wondered if, indeed, we were all federalists now.

The Senator soon grew bored with the speech and ad-libbed for twenty minutes or so, declaiming upon the dangers that "extremists of right and left" posed to "what my dear friend Arthur Schlesinger so trenchantly calls the vital center." Head throbbing with desire for the alcoholic elixir, O'Rourke recounted his heroic efforts to thwart black nationalists in the 1960s and "preserve the integrity and moral standing of the civil rights movement." He also disparaged the working-class insurgency of George Wallace as "vile demagoguery" that "had to be put down and put down hard, and by golly we did put it down!"

The craving turned to dry empty nausea, and O'Rourke hastened to find an appropriate peroration. He said, haltingly, striving for coherence, "What I hope, hope you will take with you is, is the transcendence of the system, the system, the arrangement by which the two great parties of this, this country, contend for temporary power, motivated by differing philosophies, yes, yes, different philosophies, there is a Samuel Johnson maxim, well, it escapes me at this moment, but the important thing is that the process endures, it endures attacks of gross extremists of right and left, it endures the mistakes that we, the leaders of the great parties make, it endures always, and so I salute the American Foundation for its intellectual courage, though we may not always agree, I salute you, my fellow passengers on the ship of state, the ship that shall endure, endure despite our mistakes, may it endure forever, or in the event, until it exists no more."

A rolling thunderclap of applause engulfed the auditorium. A beaming legation of Fourth Floor vice presidents led the Senator to the bar, where he absorbed a triple shot of rum with a gin chaser and with this magic tonic became the legendary Sean O'Rourke, raconteur, Irish wit, engaging barfellow, Churchillian public sage.

A coterie surrounded him, stratified by floor. The Senator laughed with boozy bonhomie at the weak jokes of the cloud people, who enveloped him with sensual delight, ecstatically breathing in the respirations of a Powerful Man. Brain trusters surrounded this inner circle, keeping respectful distance and nodding appreciatively at every vice-presidential remark. The scholars of Tijuana North formed the circle's circumference, waiting in futile hope of cornering the renowned O'Rourke and importuning him, "Meee-ster Senator O'Rourke, may I have one minute of your time to speak to you about the problems in my land of Guatem-ala?"

Attending to the potable needs of this concentric throng were the dark-skinned servants of the First Floor, the ones whom Senator O'Rourke had so valiantly empowered in his beloved early 1960s. Ah, Camelot!

Bertram and John Huey stood at the boundary separating the brain trusters from Tijuana North, listening to the cloud people swoon and flatter the great O'Rourke. They wanted desperately to drop a piercing and irreverent remark, puncturing the inflated pretensions of the grandiloquent Senator and his new admirers. But they said nothing.

O'Rourke was now fully inebriated, and his former aides Ketchum and Moost felt deeply relieved when a hapless factotum steered the Senator away from the bar and toward the exit, toward a sleep-filled night of sonorous baritone snores. Might the two escape an embarrassing reintroduction to their boss?

Alas, no.

Brain truster Teresa Terzian, a vivacious proponent of bank deregulation, intercepted the Senator and launched into an extended dirge on the Securities and Exchange Commission, which he listened to with exaggerated raptness, all the while marveling at her pulchritude and imagining lubricious and altogether undignified delights.

"Ahem, yes, yes, you certainly have a point there, miss," O'Rourke piped up whenever Miss Terzian caught her breath.

Finishing her riff, Teresa burbled, "Oh, goodness, I haven't bored you, have I?"

Before the aroused Senator could answer, Teresa caught sight of her friends Ketchum and Moost and shouted, "Oh, Senator, look here, look who's standing there, it's your faithful old aides John Huey Ketchum and Bertram Moost!"

O'Rourke followed her pointed finger and saw two anonymous young men, distinguished only by the prodigious girth of one and the horrified, ashen look of the other. Even when stupefied with liquor, the famous man knew what to do.

"My gracious," the Senator bellowed, "come over here you two. I haven't seen you for quite some time." The pair edged through the parting crowd.

"I've been wondering whatever became of you two sterling young men," the Senator lied.

John Huey smiled wanly and searched for something to say. Bertram, as ever, replied with stout composure.

"We've labored humbly in service to the republic, my good Senator. We have refined the skills learned at your estimable knee and are applying them in fealty to the same ideals that have so ennobled you. We do hope that in our labors we never dishonor you, good sir, for it was in your employ that Mr. Ketchum and I first apprehended the nature of this ship of state of which you spoke so very eloquently in your lecture."

"Ah, yes," said a befuddled O'Rourke, trying to locate his fat interlocutor in a deteriorating memory. "Yes, you're doing a superb job, from all reports, a simply superb job. Do keep it up, both of you."

The Senator clumsily patted his protégés on their shoulders, started to say something, thought better of it, and then walked to the door, waving madly at the crowd and hollering, "Great day, friends, great day, we must do this again. The vital center, guard the vital center and our mesial politicians, yes that is what we must do, keep up the good work with the Foundation."

As O'Rourke staggered out the door into the twilight chill, he glowered at his factotum and reproved him. "Why in God's fucking name didn't you extricate me earlier, you incompetent twit?"

The scolded young man did not answer. He opened the limousine door for the drunkard, who bumped his Senatorial head upon entering, which set off a round of blackguard curses.

When the Senator was deposited in his Capitol Hill townhouse, the young man drove to a nearby bar, where he met a friend and spent the nighttime hours reviling his boss with hellish oaths. "I hope some nut assassinates that son of a bitch," he slurred after six beers.

But the young man showed up for work at nine the next morning, head throbbing in migraine harmony with his boss's, and that night he drove the Senator to another affair. He continued his evening ritual night after night, performing equerry duties at dusk and drinking till midnight, and never did a complaining or defiant word pass his lips while he was in the statesman's august presence.

Meanwhile, Bertram's pompous-ass routine began to take on hardy perennial aspects. For instance, every year the European monarchist Emil de la Mortain visited DC's conservative warren, and every year Bertram dismissed the old fool (representative work: *Leftism: Genghis Khan, the Gnostic Heresy, and the New Left*) with a roll of the eyes and a knowing "Methinks EDLM never got past Filmer."

The retinue would force a nervous laugh or two, begging Providence to change the subject before their ignorance was exposed, and Bertram unfailingly obliged, serving up a nugget or two of speculation passed off as fact. (Half of Washington's men "did not prefer the company of ladies," if you believed him.)

As the booze took hold, John Huey inevitably got to wondering about Bertram's past—the one topic the raconteur never mentioned.

"Musta been an eighteen-year apprenticeship as a punching bag," John Huey once remarked of Bertram's childhood, yet a decent respect for the sanctity of youthful suffering kept him from pursuing this line of inquiry. He pictured chubby young Bertram as a young Truman Capote—at least little Capote as Hollywood liberals depicted him in the film version of *To Kill a Mockingbird*—except not as cute and ten times as delicate. Dill Harris had swung from trees, a precocious monkey. Bertram probably bawled at a hard kickball tag.

Whenever Bertram tired of holding court, or if he sensed his listener's restiveness, he'd make a grand exit, complete with overblown gestures and knowing winks, and escape to an unattended corner of the room with John Huey. (He'd grab a fistful of shrimp and pretzels when he left, dropping the overflow as he walked away. "Bertram's Indian trail," his friends called the path of crumbs and meat gobbets that spanned the separation of food table and dandy.) The two Great Right Hopes would then stand in the corner, surveying the crowd. Bertram made frequent, sweeping bows to the ladies, pretty and homely alike with Menckenesque ecumenism, and he nodded like a content old nobleman to the menfolk.

"A grand affair, wouldn't you say, JH? A grand affair indeed."

"Yeah, not so bad," replied John Huey, not willing to argue the point. "Some mighty fine poontang." He stressed the last word with demotic delight.

"Oh, indeed there is." Bertram put an extra flourish on his bow to a skinny wallflower standing alone across the room. "There are indeed some handsome *filles*."

For an Anglophile, Bertram still plunked a lot of French into his conversation. John Huey suspected he'd grow out of that as his salad days waned. By the time Bertram was thirty-five, you wouldn't be able to get a *merci* out of him with genito-electroshock.

"You in the mood for pussy tonight, Bert?"

"No, no, my good man. Don't get me wrong—these ladies are not an unattractive lot. Alas, I've yet to meet one who really captures my fancy. And how cruel of me to string some poor lass along, exciting her hopes only to dash them aground. No, no, my Lothario friend, I shan't be prowling tonight. When my heart is touched, you shall be the first to know."

With that Bertram tapped his cane on the red carpet rug, announced it was time "to do my toilet," and waddled away.

John Huey hated to see Bertram leave, for a peculiar cachet attached to the fat fop's companions. Bertram was rumored to be writing a major reformulation of Burkean conservative principles. He was a "mysterious comer," according to a *National Review* profile of "Tomorrow's Leading Men."

That Bertram's output to date comprised a handful of sloppy press releases was of no consequence; his boss at the American Foundation, for whom Bertram labored in some vague capacity, called his protégé's work-in-progress "a strong hint of a peerless mind at work—a genius, really, eccentric in personal habits but a figure who will be of immense use to the cause of ordered liberty and public virtue."

No one, save his boss, had ever glimpsed Bertram's incubating opus, and inquiries were met with an arched eyebrow and an enigmatic, "We shall see, we shall most certainly see."

John Huey hated to lose Bertram's company for a more intimate reason as well. Now, when he stood alone at a party, he felt that all eyes were upon him, mocking his ineptness at the courting arts. Bertram tolerated, even encouraged John Huey's boastful façade of hotshot lecher. There was a tacit agreement between the friends: John Huey's empty sexual braggadocio was treated as fact; Bertram's lofty celibacy went unexamined.

Bertram's leaving breached the contract. To the rest of the party, John Huey was an average-looking smartass who always came stag and exited loaded and alone. (Kara, as is her ilk's wont, never materialized.) When other revelers looked at him, did they see the swaggering young conservative star that Bertram allowed him to be? Or were they staring, with a mixture of pity and contempt, at a footloose bachelor whose only sexual contact had been a humiliating premature ejaculation inside the half-conscious Lassy Dean half a decade ago?

He wished his naked self invisible, and the only way he knew to conceal it was alcohol. So he'd booze it up, on the theory that girls prefer guys who stammer out of drunkenness rather than nervousness. He could never confirm the hypothesis, and he wondered if his consistent failure at parties might even disprove it.

Awaiting the commencement of yet another summer night's party, John Huey sat on a wooden bench in DuPont Circle, shifting his ass from slat to slat, avoiding numbness. His gaze drifted rightward. Two young black men stared intently at their chessboard. A lonely queer, haggard and emaciated, lay on the grass, sobbing, lost in some private inferno. A fat white woman in a Peoples Drug Store uniform was reading, now and then mechanically reaching into a bag of popcorn. An old bum slept next to a pine trashbasket, snoring through a meandering sermon that a rotund, drunken old Cotton Mather was declaiming to no one in particular. Car horns honked impatiently as their drivers snaked around the circle, then shot out into the feeder avenues.

A tiny roach, diligent and purposeful, traversed the cement sidewalk at John Huey's feet. As it scurried into the penumbra of his shadow, he stamped his sneaker on it. The gesture was more thoughtless than wanton.

A primitive roar jerked John Huey to attention.

"What-so-evvvver-you-do," thundered the besotted hulk whose powerful, gaping strides carried him to John Huey's bench, "to the *least* of my brothers, that . . . you . . . do . . . unto ME."

The preacher drew a breath. John Huey sat up straight and swallowed the accumulating saliva in his mouth. He was scared, even though he sat in a public park in dusky light, in full view of dozens of consanguineous nomad souls.

"You have sto-len the life of God's littlest creature, sir. Do you believe that God has expelled that midge from His dominion, or do you believe that God has ex-empt-ed you, sir, from the reach of His law?"

Fear of assault fading, John Huey studied the preacher. He was a white man of indeterminate age, massive and powerful in chest and arms, despite the ravages of booze. His breath was strongly redolent of Sweet Ripple wine. John Huey focused on the evangel's eyes—thick, mucusy, bulbous orbs, slivers of blood red racing across the immense whitenesses that protruded from his sockets, the widest reticulae he'd ever seen.

Scrutiny dispelled fear. The preacher was a common bum; a quarter ought to propitiate him. John Huey was emboldened.

"Get the fuck away from me, I'm busy. Here's a quarter," he said, tossing the coin on the bench to avoid hand contact.

The sermonizer's monstrous eyes looked to the sky. He threw his arms upward, the left elbow grazing John Huey's chin.

"Forgive him, Lord, he knows not what he does when he takes Your blessed name in vain. He is a foolish and ignorant child, as were all Your humble servants, the holy apostles of Christendom."

The preacher turned back to his quarry. "Thou shalt NEVER take the Lord's name in vain," he lectured, a spasm of righteous fury convulsing his twitching left eye. "It is so written."

John Huey, unaffrighted, decided to have a little fun.

"Where is that written? What kind of egotistical God places blasphemy on the same moral plane as murder?

When's the last time you read the Bible? You'd sell your motherfucking soul for a gulp of the vintage where the grapes of wrath are stored. You don't fool me."

The preacher pondered this, unaffronted. His voice fell several octaves, his facial wattles rippled, then relaxed. He was pleased that someone had engaged him in conversation. When he spoke, it was in a slow monotone.

"It is true, my skeptical friend, that I drink. That my raiment is torn. That I sleep with the rats. That I have whored. That I have been faithless to family. That I have taken the Lord's name in vain more times than can be forgiven. To a man such as yourself, I must appear pitiful or grotesque or even humorous."

John Huey regretted the insult and tried to apologize, but the preacher's address was inexorable. He had something to say, and he was going to say it.

"I will not pretend that I am as virtuous a man as you. That would be a prideful sin, a sin of vanity, and my platter is full enough already. I do not desire to sin again in my life. But I will say this, sir: I will say that you are no better than the gentleman lying yonder. [He pointed to the drowsy hobo.] You are both created in God's image, though you may not choose to believe so."

John Huey smirked, anticipating a fusillade of liberal pieties. A crusader for the sainted homeless . . . *aaargh!*

The preacher, however, was no flaccid do-gooder.

"I suspect," he continued, "that you attribute your lofty station in this life to talent and skill and worthy industriousness. You believe yourself to be wise, very wise, wiser than men twice your age, wiser than men half your age, wiser than men dead and wiser than men yet unborn. Wiser, forsooth, then the gentleman sleeping on the soil yonder. Yes, much wiser than the gentleman who sleeps on the soil. His failure was ordained by God; so, too, was your success. Such is your view, I venture, and perhaps such is the view of our friend who drools into the glebe.

"I shall not try to change your mind or give you moral instruction. What can a drunkard and wastrel such as I teach a man of your caliber? I will simply say this, and leave you with this, and you may reflect upon it or reject it. Such is your right. I once occupied a position of considerable earthly importance in this town, long ago, in another age. Men and women of influence and breeding courted me. I lived in comfort, in splendor one might say, and I did enjoy the feast of plenty that I took to be my just desert. Then one day the sun rose, as it had since the days of Genesis, only on that day I did not feel its warmth. It ambled across the sky as if it were a great painting, there for me to observe but never to take succor from. I assumed, in my ignorance, that the error was the sun's, and all would return to normal, and the correctness of the universe would be restored when the sun discovered its error. But the next day the sun rose again, and again I did not feel its warmth. Day upon day upon day the sun rose, but never once did it share its heat with me. It did not heed me. It did not heed me for many years, despite my pleas and promises and the vilest oaths that man's mouth can utter. Until one day, in this park, my bones weary and my spirit fatigued, I lay my head down to sleep at the root of a maple tree, and in the morning, in the brand new dawn, I felt the comforting rays of the sun caress my face, just as they had years ago and just as they have ever since. And today, sir, the sun looks to me just as it did on that spring morning forty years ago, at the start of my long journey. It will look the same forty years hence, I know. And I can assure you that no exertion, no labor, no plan, no solemn pledge, not even a bargain with the Evil One will change things. You are not the master of this world, sir, and the sun will never seek your counsel. I bid you a new day."

With that, the preacher unsheathed a pint of cheap rum, swilled a prodigious swig, and stormed away.

4

Every Washington asshole and his brother writes a syndicated column. The pundits—would-be *philosophes* who scratch out a scarecrow subsistence, $50 to $100 per the two, four, eight jerkwater dailies that carry them—churn out their eight-hundred-word cogitations each week, iterating and reiterating the proper, polite conservative or liberal dogma, depending upon which coat of assumptions the tyro sage feels more comfortable wearing.

John Huey won his column after a nine-month apprenticeship in the American Foundation's PR office. His releases and bulletins showed flashes of life, at least when contrasted with the deadened prose of the True Believers who shared his office. So a Foundation VP asked the Solley News Service to take a look at the kid: "A promising new voice of young America, the America that elected Ronald Reagan and is taking over the college campuses," bloviated the VP in his letter to the crabbed shrew Ellen Solley.

After a sample column ("Doin' the Deregulation Dance," the VP's title—"Old bag Solley wants to reach young people," he reasoned), John Huey had a new job and an embarrassing new Solley-supplied sobriquet: "The Promising New Voice of Young America." A dorky picture was duly taken and sent out with a column.

The shtick worked. *Vox post-pubescia* climbed steadily through pundit ranks his first year, peaking at thirty-nine regular outlets and never hitting fewer than thirty-five. He'd ascended well above his ground-bound colleagues, but the stratosphere—two hundred-plus papers—was mercilessly remote. John Huey wanted to deliver his encyclicals on network TV, after all, and thirty-five mostly fly-over papers wouldn't sweep *Meet the Press*'s floors.

Like most columnists, John Huey wrote in a vacuum, seldom receiving plaudits or complaints. A large Eastern paper's editorial page editor wrote Solley that "Ketchum seems to have swallowed whole the King James version of the College Republican platform, and damned if he isn't excreting it chunk by chunk every week. Not in our paper."

And his disparagements of feminism ("Madam and Eve, the gym teacher and the NOW preacher," were a favorite fictive couple) rankled the usual suspects.

But John Huey lacked the exposure one needs to be an authentic controversialist. He tried picking fights with famous politicians and his better-known cogitating kin; his targets ignored him, as an elephant does a pesky mosquito. He solicited puff lines from friends and strangers for a mass mailing to Ketchum-less papers, but the shiniest paean he got—"bluntest Neanderthal stylist since Westbrook Pegler laid down his club"—came from an elderly Idaho editor long associated with the John Birch Society. He flooded the networks and talk shows with clips, some politely acknowledged, most rudely shitcanned.

But he kept on the treadmill, writing aggressive if orthodox polemics, sending "Voice of Young America" kits to recalcitrant editors and the unheeding media elite, eatingbreathingdrinkingsleeping his column while visions of networks and Lippmann and Mencken and seducing ambassadors' wives danced in his head.

The transmutative properties of time spare no one, not even the beloved grandparent. After his death Fred's rough, refractory nature grew tamer by the minute in John Huey's mind. He came to see Fred's enthusiasm for Huey Long and Share Our Wealth and Every Man a King as the fanciful, almost charming notions of an ignorant but well-meaning janitor. John Huey found himself shedding any reservations about his forebear's sentiments, going so far as to invoke Fred as a kind of populist totem behind which he could slip into the enemy camp and slit a row of throats before the poor bastards knew what hit 'em.

"My grandpappy Fred Ketchum used to say. . . ."

"A duplicitous sleaze like X might fool the striped-pants boys, but he'd not pass a plug nickel off on my Grandpa. . . ."

"My grandpappy, an old Huey Long man, woulda thunk it this way. . . ."

"You don't get right back up after you been knocked on yer can, you gonna stick to the ground."

John Huey minted that apothegm on a drizzly Thursday afternoon, crediting it to his wise old Grandpa Fred in his column. He repeated it often, drew solace from it, mustered resolve at its articulation. It became, in the fullness of time, a favorite motto. But the first time he attributed this apocryphal quote to Fred, John Huey felt a mite queasy. He paced his office, sitting at the word processor for a few seconds, reading the lie, attacking the frog that always blocked his throat when he hit an ethical impasse. Then he bolted from the newly upholstered swivel chair, setting it a-swirlin' as he strode the length of his workplace, cussing and phlegm-wrestling, unable to focus on the issue at hand, incapable of discerning a clear mental image of Fred, unwilling to ask the ghost in his head questions about honesty, probity, and the line between venerating and traducing the dead.

He struggled for an hour, pathetic and futile, annoyed that his goddam grandfather didn't have the horse sense to say what John Huey said he'd said. For a moment he tried to convince himself that Fred really *had* coined the epigram in question, but this mendacity was too much even for a falling man.

"Fuck it," John Huey sputtered, and he modemed his

copy, lie and all, to the syndicate. He grabbed his coat, averted his eyes from the 4-by-6 black-and-white photo of Fred that was taped to the wall, and went out and got good and drunk.

The call came on a sticky Friday morning at summer's end.

"Hi, Mr. Ketchum," piped a lass with a dry, briny Connecticut accent. "This is Alison Hassett with *Face the Nation*."

"Oh, hi, how you doin'?" John Huey had talked to network production footsoldiers before; they'd ask a couplathree inane questions, be nonplussed by simple and clear answers, then stutter an "Uh, thanks for your help," and hang up.

"Fine, thank you." (Alison dated Groton men, he felt sure.) "Mr. Ketchum, we've read a number of your columns, especially on racial issues, and quite frankly we have been impressed. This Sunday our show is focusing on the changing racial agenda. We'd like you to appear as a guest. Might that be possible?"

Oh, Saint Alison! Providence hath shone its radiant light upon my wretched and undeserving head, chanted John Huey. (He'd misquoted John Winthrop in yesterday's column and was stuck in a bastardized Puritan vulgate.) The Solley crowd was going to flip: youth's smiling avatar was going network.

"Of course, it's possible," he spit into the phone. "When should I be there?"

"Oh, by ten-thirty Sunday morning, so our makeup crew can give you the once-over. You'll be sharing the show's final ten-minute block with a representative of one of the major civil rights groups, TBA, OK?"

"Sure, sure," he assured her. "I'll be there, ten-thirty Sunday morning."

"Super."

"I'm looking forward to it."

"Super," she repeated. "The studio's on the sixth floor. Goodbye."

John Huey jumped up, flailed his arms, shook his head with joyous ferocity, and mouthed a primal silent scream (the walls were papier-mâché thin). "Oh, man," he burbled seven or eight times. "Man oh man oh man oh man."

He paced the room hyperactively, smacking his fist into his palm every few seconds and incanting "man oh man oh man oh man" while visions of sagehood and celebrity hung in the air, in front of the electronic Tantalus.

He paced and chanted for an hour. His body surged with invigorating lifeblood, the way it did when he'd witness an inspiring athletic feat on TV and place himself in the hero's role. (How many times had he hit Carlton Fisk's extra-inning foul-pole hanger?) *Face the Nation* was John Huey's diving fingertip catch of the last-second long bomb.

"Man oh man oh man oh man."

As euphoria settled into suffused contentment, he started calling around, a vainglorious egghead inviting friends to the weekend's joust.

David Krull, the overdecorous Solley VP who supervised

his columns: "Why, John Huey, that is *marvelous* news. Absolutely marvelous. I think you'll agree that the boost this can provide your column is . . . quite . . . large. I shall call Mrs. Solley right this instant. Oh, this makes my weekend."

Bob Paul, inveterate Moonie junketeer and twelve-paper pundit hacker: "Fanfuckingtastic! *Face the Fucking Nation.* Man, you have got a viselike grip on the world's scrotum. Squeeze them balls, man. Fanfuckingtastic!"

Finally, he called Bertram Moost. "Superb news, my good man. Television needs its Belloc."

"Yeah. Say, Bert, what do you think the pussy ramifications of my lionization will be?"

"Hmmm," pondered Bertram. "Considerable, I'd hazard. You'll not be lacking in conjugal company, my friend. No, sir, indeedy. Cherchez la femme, old friend."

"You gonna watch?"

"Most certainly. Most certainly. My revivification of Mr. Burke will lose half an hour's time, but the viewing will have its rewards, I'd wager."

"You bet your ass. Sunday, eleven-thirty A.M., be there."

"Righto."

"Bye."

On his way out, John Huey stopped at the worn and torn photo of Fred tacked to his wall. Fred stared straight and square at the camera. Two windblown snowdrifts flanked him; a dusky moon rose over his shoulder.

"Hi, Grandpa." John Huey's long-inactive tear ducts stirred. "I'm gonna be on TV Sunday. I'm probably not gonna say what you'd say, but I hope. . . ."

He felt silly and self-conscious. For Christ's sake, Fred's picture was just an optical image of a dead man graven on photosensitive paper, spiked to a plaster wall. Talking to a rock was every bit as rational and productive. Superstition, sheeesh.

Sunday came, at long last. John Huey was being interviewed on National Television. Questions—trite questions, but questions all the same—were being asked. With a serious mien, the Voice of Young America was offering measured, thoughtful responses.

His mouth and brain were on autopilot, molding and speaking the boilerplate simultaneously, each line a solid, sensible, complete sentence. "When you tax something, you get less of it. When you subsidize that same thing, you get more of it."

In the early stages of his career, John Huey had secretly cherished every such bromide. His pedantry was antiphonic—the cynical imp in his mind mocked the triteness and idiot certitude of his pronouncements, hurling the same contemptuous expression at each banality: "A young Daniel Webster! A young Daniel Webster! A young Daniel Webster!"

The voice, he knew, was that of his grandfather, though Fred hadn't a touch of the heavy sarcasm that passed for wit in John Huey. How would the old man have reacted to John Huey's responses? Not with anger, disgust, nor even manifest disappointment, for Fred loved his own—despite their venial, mortal, or eternally damning sins—and even John Huey's snarling evocations of Huey Long and Share Our Wealth—"Who wants to share his wealth with every scheming welfare bimbo capable of signing her name on the dotted line?"—couldn't have ruffled the old coot's craggy, loving serenity.

But now, platitudes dripping from his mouth, John Huey felt the fright of the entertainer in the glare of the spotlight. He was boring his audience, and he knew it.

His foeman, via satellite, had turned out to be Walter Thomas, a career Negro of the most reprehensible sort: born into the Atlanta black bourgeoisie, M.A. in Establishment Negritude from Fisk, fetched Dr. King a cup of coffee and invariably teared up as he recalled a slightly embellished version of their encounter. ("He looked at me—right through me almost, 'cause Martin had the most penetrating eyes I've ever seen—and he said 'Thank you, brother. You know, I hear the angels calling my name, calling my weary bones home. I could die, be assassinated, at any moment, in any place. And I will take to my grave and to my home up above the glorious memory of this favor that you have done for me.'") Thomas had labored in the vineyards of bureaucracy ever since.

Walter was giving the hostess the same shopworn rap he'd been performing since he mau-mau'd his first white liberal. "Two hundred years of slavery," "economic apartheid," "*Fun-da-men-tal* disagreements." Blahblahblah.

Against this black blowhard John Huey fired, rat-a-tat-tat, the right-wing shibboleths that served as his fixed and unchanging arsenal. "Economic opportunity," "up by the bootstraps," "subsidizing poverty." Blahblahblah.

Young Daniel Webster fencing with young Frederick Douglass.

As Thomas undertook a disquisition on "the compassion gap," a crouching staffer darted onto the set, slipped a note into the hostess's hand, and fled whence he came. She read it, folded it, and tossed it under the table.

"Mr. Thomas," she interposed between banalities, "Mr. Ketchum has written the following in his syndicated column. Quote: 'The simple, unvarnished truth is that most people on welfare are deep-down lazy.' Endquote. Do you agree?"

Thomas adjusted his tortoiseshell glasses, which had slid halfway down his nose, sighed a sigh of sanctimonious resignation, and attacked.

"If Mr. Ketchum really wrote that, he is at best a fool, at worst. . . ." He left the implication dangling. "I speak for the black people of this nation, the unemployed black people of this nation, when I say that work equals dignity, no work equals no dignity. Give us jobs, and we will work, and we will contribute to this nation."

A typically jejune response, thought John Huey, who figured that time was a-wasting and Grandpa Fred better be invoked, the sooner the better. He ransacked his head for an anecdote: genuine articles need not apply.

But the hostess sensed a dramatic light at the end of the tunnel—racial controversy!—and she bore in. "Mr. Ketchum, you've heard Mr. Thomas call you a fool at best, a . . . something else . . . at worst. How would you respond?"

Not exactly a deft interrogation, but the show had been resuscitated.

"Well," started John Huey, a pseudodrawl creeping into his voice, "I used to have a Grandpappy, name of Fred Ketchum, he was an organizer in upstate New York for Huey Long, the Kingfish, the Louisiana populist who was, figuratively if not literally, colorblind, and my Grandpappy often said...."

"That's all to the good, but what about workfare?" the hostess interrupted.

The non sequitur knocked John Huey off balance. He forgot the anecdote he was about to tell; frantically, he racked his brain for a tale, an axiom, an aphorism, a cliché, even a lie about workfare and blacks. He remembered a dusty right-wing saw belying the "government jobs promote dignity" canard. He opened his mouth to repeat it, and in that recondite and sublime second at which the thought becomes the statement and the shapeless mass of a million brain impulses is articulated with remarkable precision and clarity, something snapped. A ghost entered the machine. And the darkest, most remote recesses of John Huey's mind substituted an alternative articulation of those formless thoughts. He intoned, "You can lead a nigger to workfare, but you can't make...."

"WHAT did he say?" screamed Thomas, a thousand miles away. The hostess sat dumb, speechless, watching Thomas's four-inch head shake vigorously, spastically, on the monitor. His livid image was cartoonish, a wild melange of shaken fists and shouted insults and ill-considered threats that vanished into a video bell jar, never to be seen, transcribed, or microfiched. The network had cut to a commercial—four minutes worth of commercials and promotions, in fact—seconds after the N-word had been spoken. The show was ended; John Huey's was the last word.

———

The monitors blanked.

The hostess whipsnapped her neck, an unconscious fashion-model tic that set in motion a fluid undulation of row upon row of gorgeously configured blond hair. When her golden locks had settled, she gathered her notebook and a yellow legal pad on which an underpaid subaltern had written out capsule summaries of the guests and suggested questions.

If John Huey had filched the pad he'd have seen a neat, felt-tipped scrawl reading: JOHN HUEY KETCHUM IS A CONSERVATIVE COLUMNIST. HE WILL DISAGREE WITH MR. THOMAS ON RACIAL ISSUES. ASK HIM. . . . and on it went, step-by-step instructions to the millionaire marionette on whom multitudes relied for whatever news the powers-that-be deemed suitable for citizen viewing.

John Huey sat, outwardly calm, his innards in roiled panic. His mind dredged up the memory of a long-forgotten photo of his youth—a murderer, head shaved, eyes ablaze with oracular dread, the beatific fear of a visionary who has just witnessed his own horrible and imminent—and immanent?—death. The murderer was wearing a death-row workshirt, and a prison guard was leading him—no, he actually appeared to be *accompanying* him—to what John Huey supposed was the electric chair or execution line or, worst of all, the benevolent tomb known as the gas chamber.

The guard was a thick, stolid man, like most of his confreres a local fellow walking in his father's and grandfather's footsteps. What John Huey remembered most about this photo—what haunted his dreams for weeks afterward—was the odd way the doomed man's line of sight intersected that of the pale, obviously frightened guard. They were looking at the same thing, far beyond the mechanical eye of the astigmatic camera, and little John Huey was paralyzed by the thought that he, too, would someday see the mysterious apparition that rendered a killer and his jailer ashen, ghostly, terrified.

"G'day." The clipped, brusque farewell of the hostess snapped John Huey from his reverie. She left the stage, and he sat alone, clearing his throat, the thin screech of a moving camera dolly and the insistent whirring of the crew's coffeemaker the only sounds.

A production assistant—the plump young woman who'd fetched water for John Huey in the waiting room—efficiently and wordlessly detached his mike. She did not look at him, and when he tried to speak his first syllable dissolved into a pukey cough.

John Huey rose, mesmerized (though by what he did not know), and sleepwalked to the elevator. He pushed the Down button dozens of times, senselessly, until the doors opened and he felt himself freefalling, straining at gravity, trapped in another plummeting elevator dream. Then he was standing outside the CBS building on M Street.

When John Huey tried later to recall his flight, his most salient memory was that no one looked at him, no one paid a shred of attention to the instant pariah. He wondered why the opposite did not occur: why a lynch mob had not formed, why no member of the aggrieved race had spit on him or coldcocked him or acted the proud, dignified, affronted Sidney Poitier Hollywood Negro.

John Huey ran home, pinstriped suit flapping in the late August breeze. He lifted his phone off its hook and dived into bed, shaking, quavering, frightened out of his wits. He curled into the fetal position, drooling like a baby onto his pillow linen, and he lay there till nightfall, a cowering 150-pound infant dreading the morning light, afraid of the inevitable egress from his room, his refuge, into a world whose prey he had become in one horrific moment.

5

He arrived at work early Monday morning.

When he flicked on the light in his office, John Huey half expected to illumine a bare room, stripped to a utilitarian chair or two and the primordial dented gray file cabinets that depress white-collar workers in every hamlet and parish across the USA. But the room looked just as he had left it.

"Lazy stagehands," thought John Huey, and he tried to twin "mise en scene" with "Ludwig von Mises" to make a joke, unsuccessfully of course. The blinking red light of his answering machine distracted his eye.

One . . . two . . . three . . . four . . . five . . . six . . . seven . . . eight . . . nine . . . ten . . . eleven. . . . Stop and repeat. Eleven calls.

He weakly sought to stem the incoming tide of nausea by thinking of eleven-letter-words that described his position.

Crestfallen. Despondency. Hopelessness was too long, ostracized too short. Up shit creek, Fred's sole vulgar locution, fit just fine.

John Huey tossed his tweed jacket on the undersized visitor's chair (an intimidation trick gleaned from one of those looking-out-for-#1 books he hid behind Hayek on his bookshelf). He dismissed the "Erase! Erase!" temptation and punched the Rewind button, sank into his chair (pretty damn plush, he thought), placed his fists on his temples, and listened.

The sibilant tape stopped rewinding. *Click*. Then came the static that auspicates the Play mode.

"Uh, hi, JH, it's Karl. I guess I'll talk to you Monday. Have a good weekend. Bye."

What a nice gesture by the gods, the doomed man thought. A tease of reprieve. Could all eleven be Friday night calls?

No.

"John Huey, this is David Krull, please call me at six-nine-four four-four-hundred." The syndicate. Après Krull, the deluge.

"Racist muthafucka!" *Click*.

"I said cocksuckin' white boy racist muthafucka!" A harmless kid, speculated John Huey. Come on, kid, call seven more times.

"Mr. Ketchum, this is Marlene Salter with the *New York Post*. I've been calling you at home but getting no answer.

Please call me at seven-six-seven three-two-four-oh or six-two-six two-one hundred."

"Yeah, John, this is Bob. Are you outta your mind or what? Man, are you in deep shit. Talk to ya Monday." Ah, the soothing, dulcet tones of a friend and fellow half-assed columnist.

"This is C. L. Narvaez of the *San Francisco Examiner*. Please call me at four-four-three two-oh-seven-seven or tomorrow at five-four-seven thirteen-forty-five. Thank you very much."

"Even the buffoon Long had the sense to maledict the white man's burden in the privacy of the salon and the saloon. I shall talk to you, my good boor, on the morrow." It was the first time Bertram had ever left a message on John Huey's answering machine.

Two hang-ups followed. "One more call," John Huey said to himself, nearly adding, "and I'm out of the woods."

"This is Ann Nanni of the *Buffalo News*. I just wanted to let you know personally that we are dropping your column and that I'm sorry we picked it up in the first place." Dead air for five, ten seconds, as she collected her thoughts. "You know, I never understood your political views in the first place. You were sold to us as a conservative, and we needed one, and we liked the first piece you sent us, about Russia or something. But then you got kind of boring and stuffy, to tell the truth, and this Grandpa Fred hick stuff was really . . . *cloying*, I guess is the word, and syrupy, and to tell the truth I don't even believe you have a Grandpa Fred, 'cause if you did you wouldn't be the way you are. . . . I don't know if the machine's still running, if it isn't I guess I'm just talking into the air, but if it is I want to let you know that you're a crummy person. Plus you use these big words that you probably don't know what they mean anyhow. So good-bye."

In desperation, John Huey sat down before his word processor and began to compose his next column.

AN APOLOGY
John Huey Ketchum
Solley News Service

I have sinned, Lord, have I sinned, and I shall reap the bitter consequences of my actions.

For those of you who were out raking the leaves, prepping little Jason for his kindergarten cheese-tasting debut, or stamping license plates at the local pen, let me explain my transgression.

Last Sunday yours truly, the baddest cat ever to emerge from Batavia, New York, made his debut on television's *Face the Nation.* Yes, the hostess is as toothsome in person as she is on the idiot box. No, I don't think she'll be inviting me back any time soon.

You see, I erred grievously—no, I *sinned*—during our colloquy. Your correspondent was pontificating on the state of politics, western civilization, and the designated hitter rule when one of my fellow guests started a rant-and-rave about the *plight* of America's minorities.

"There is no room at the inn for citizens of African origin," he began, allegorically, and we proceeded to duke it out over the state of the "civil rights" movement. The talk turned to workfare, and before I knew what was happening, a vile sentence came barreling out of my mouth. No need to repeat it: suffice to say that it contained the epithet "nigger."

Nothing I do, or say, no public act of expiation, can atone for my misstatement. It's inexcusable. For what it's worth, I apologize and ask all my readers, black, white, red, and yellow, to find in their hearts some measure of forgiveness. If not today, perhaps tomorrow, next month, next year.

Nothing left to say, I guess. Except an apology of a private, personal nature.

Regular readers are familiar with my late grandfather, Fred Ketchum. Old Fred used to tell me, during our long fall drives through the ripened orchards of the Genesee Valley, of a black friend of his named Jesse Lawrence.

Fred and Jesse used to travel the back roads of upper New York, proselytizing for Louisiana's colorful Governor and Senator, Huey Long. Now, nights are cold in New York's highlands, yet more than once Fred lay himself down to sleep on his padded rucksack, eyes fixed on the shimmery light of the stars.

You see, a number of New York innkeepers wouldn't shelter a black, no matter how much green was offered. And Fred wouldn't sleep in a snug racist bed while his buddy froze on the ground.

"What was the point?" a relative once asked Fred.

"Refusing to accept lodging didn't make Jesse any warmer, it just got you a bed of rocks and dirt."

Fred smiled, patient with his blind kinsman. "Don't you see," he said, "I'd have lost my dignity if I betrayed ole Jesse. And a man ain't got dignity, no bed is gonna warm his soul."

I'm sorry, Fred; I'm sorry, Jesse; I'm sorry, readers.

John Huey sat in his swivel chair, chewing his blue pen cap, occasionally fondling himself like a nervous little boy.

His column had been sent to his thirty-five regular customers, plus twenty or so irregulars, almost a week ago. Today David Krull would call, give John Huey the final pickup tally, and deliver a pronunciamento on the future of last year's Edna G. Grabley Freedom Award–winning columnist.

A friend or two had phoned with perfunctory exhortations of the keep-your-chin-up variety. Too, he'd received a letter from Anaheim, California, chastising him for a "craven wimp-out to the racialists of the left," and whatever that meant at least it confirmed the appearance of his message of contrition in the *Orange County Register*. Things were getting back to normal, he thought, and once David confirmed the expected damage—eight, maybe ten drops—the affair would be yesterday's contretemps.

As he manipulated the pen cap across his dental arch, John Huey caught a glimpse of Fred's yellowing photo. He felt the tiniest pang of guilt. Not shame, mind you, but the nettling guilt of the naughty child who's fooled his favorite teacher with a fake doctor's note.

The Fred-and-Jesse story, after all, was bullshit. A fabrication, a web of lies, a farrago of mistruths, an audacious misrepresentation of his grandfather's very essence. A queering of his quiddity.

Fred had no Negro friends, at least as far as John Huey knew. If Fred ever ran into Jesse, he'd have called him "nigger"; if Fred had owned that inn, Jesse'd have frozen his black ass off.

The imp in John Huey took over, teasing the concocter of the lie. "Why Jesse? Why not Leroy? Rastus? Remus? Why not Uncle Ben? Uncle Tom? Why not Fred's wife Jemima, who like de jellyroll berry much massah? Why didn't Fred and Jemima have young uns, why wasn't her granchile named John Huey? Why didn't her quadroon granchile summon turbaned Saint Jemima in his defense against the slanderous charge of racism?"

"Hell, boy, if you'da claimed black blood the archangels of affirmative-action liberalism would've searched posthaste for that quarter or eighth of your form that was tan and tawny so's they could kiss it in abject veneration. It's called niggerolatry."

John Huey floored his high dudgeon. He betook a defense of his Fred distortions.

"Look, the lie is a tested tool of politics. What is history but the lies and propaganda of the dominant class and reigning empires? Kennedy paid Sorensen to write *Profiles in Courage*; the Japs only bombed Pearl Harbor 'cause we embargoed them and cut off their oil; and Huey Long was born to middle-class, slightly decaying gentry, not some hardscrabble farmhands. History has no real, corporeal existence—it's gone, it's past, it's lighter than air, it's a market of fictions from which we pick and choose, taking whatever can improve our lives or complement the self-portraits we all paint. Fred is dead. Why not use his life as compost for mine? I honor him in the remembrance, and if his paper existence is cleaner, smoother, less coarse than the flesh-and-bones Fred, who's to say he'd not be grateful for the burnishing? No, accuser, take back your guilt; I didn't do a damn thing wrong. I gave Fred life after death, I resurrected him, breathed life into his chalky, forgotten corpse, and if I want to wipe the gravy stains off his tie I'll do it, and if I want to rusticate him and make him a sage I'll do that too, and if I think his politics and social views could use a little updating, why I'll do that as well. My conscience is free, and my beloved Grandpa is alive."

The phone rang.

"John Huey, this is David Krull," enunciated the mannered, minced voice at the phone's other end. "I have two things to tell you."

John Huey cleared his throat, suddenly diffident. Krull—the mocked, reviled, ineffectual Krull—had become omniscient and omnipotent.

"Yes, David, how are ya? Good to hear from ya. I was just. . . ."

Krull cut him off with a newfound confident brusqueness.

"The figures are in. Your apology failed. Only four papers picked it up, and two did so while apprising us of their intention to drop your column starting next week, and of course mathematics teaches us that four minus two equals two."

For a moment John Huey pondered Krull's wordiness—"gotta use the word 'periphrastic' in a column," he told himself—and he wondered if Krull read his phone conversations from a script, as a long-gone intern had once alleged.

"I think you'll agree that two papers is an insufficient total for a syndicated columnist. It's not profitable for us, and I'm sure it's embarrassing for you. Therefore, I regret to inform you that we're removing your name from our roster, effective immediately. You will receive severance pay equivalent to two weeks of pickups at your old rate. Do you have any questions?"

An image of Krull's pockmarked face, ravaged by adolescent pimples and boils and pustules, flooded John Huey's mind. Krull was bathed in warm, saffron sunlight, each scarred pore a seething, turbulent, independent ecosystem.

"Uh, I . . ." John Huey cleared his throat, erasing the Krullian chimera. He hadn't any idea what to say.

"I . . . listen, David, maybe a few weeks and maybe this'll blow over . . . a temporary storm if we just batten down the hatches. I've wanted to do a piece for *National Review* on the Democratic left, a long piece, four, five thousand words. Why don't I just take a leave of absence and do that? It ought to be controversial as hell, char a few red asses, if you know what I mean, and then when the storm clouds pass I'll resume. . . ."

"No, John Huey, you will not resume your column, not with the Solley News Service. I wish you the best, but our relationship is finished. You'll receive your severance check in two or three days. Then that's it. We expect the return of all equipment, of course."

"Uh. . . ."

"Good-bye, John Huey. I'm sorry it ended this way. I truly am."

Apostasy pays, at least in the brownstone circles of Washington's intell-pol community. For some unfathomable reason, a writer's views are invested with a sobering weight if the pundit claims to have once pitched his tent in a rival camp.

A communist turned conservative is lionized for sagacity born of experience, for peerless intellectual probity, for a rigorous, unsentimental mind, all because he was once fool enough to profess faith in Joe Stalin or Fidel Castro or Mao Tse-Tung or any other devil who speaks the language of progressivism.

John Huey had condemned these "Convenient Commies," as he'd called them in an early column. And he had once written a lengthy investigative piece exposing the majority of the bumptious converts as liars, pale self-promoters whose closest encounter with the real left was jerking their teen-aged joints to sexy pictures of Elizabeth Gurley Flynn. Plus they were a humorless lot, always prating about the Max Shachtman–Norman Thomas rift and how the KGB was manipulating Fijian elections. As much as John Huey hated Reds, he just couldn't work up much outrage over Henry Wallace's refusal to repudiate the CPUSA.

"Revisionists of the Right," he'd titled his exposé, and he had been proud of it. John Huey had offered the piece to a major nonpartisan journal of ideas. He'd celebrated its acceptance with a six-pack and a shivering midnight window-shopping walk down 14th Street, Washington's tenderloin. The essay marked him as a serious man, he thought, no mere dasher-off of eight-hundred-word causeries.

A few weeks later, while he was scouting for misprints in the galleys, a brief note arrived, encased in a Federal Express package. The sender was a dour, thirtyish polemicist whose fabrications about his "leftist" past John Huey had mercilessly documented.

John Huey tore open the envelope with pregnant glee, expecting a whiny, importunate letter. He began to read.

DEAR MR. KETCHUM:
I have read your shameless attack on anticommunists. You're a KGB agent's dream: a useful idiot of the right. As a stupid son of brawling frontier populists, you will understand why I am commissioning a private investigation of your family past, to be published in *Commentary*. I expect to find your "Grandpappy Fred Ketchum" and others to be who you say they are, consistent with the breathless descriptions in your columns. If not, you will read about it.
SINCERELY,
Joshua W. Perlitz
Committee to Defend the Western World

John Huey had called the magazine's editor that afternoon, mumbling something about "personal problems of an extremely grave nature," and how he was very sorry but he'd have to pull the article from consideration. The editor's initial confusion never erupted into full-fledged anger or even exasperation, thanks to the ominously ambiguous nature of John Huey's excuse. "Personal problems of an extremely grave nature" hinted so strongly at brain aneurysms and inoperable tumors and dead spouses that John Huey would forevermore use it to beg off unpleasant duties.

Now, alack, his once-bright star had dimmed and was falling rapidly to earth. When it hit terra it would bore into the ground with breathtaking velocity, through rocks and streams and ore deposits, through crust and epidermis and into the planet's dull, suffocating center, where the promising young polemicist would die a quick, unmourned death.

He had one last hope. It came to him when he found "Revisionists of the Right" while cleaning out his files.

Left to right, left to right, left to right—the natural order of things political. A swarm of snotty little intellectuals had trudged the beaten-down path from left to right and spent the rest of their lives boring readers with their lyncean insights. Hell, weren't half of *National Review*'s founding editors ex-reds?

But what about right to left? Where were the countercyclical travelers, what books contained their stories? And wouldn't the left love to get its grasping hands on a right-wing turncoat, parading him before cameras, equipping him for battle, offering him a column at a livable wage?

Mebbe so, mebbe no. No harm in trying.

The chickenshit liberals of the Democratic establishment wouldn't piss on him if he was dying of thirst, he was sure of that. They looked askance at *any* writer who aspired beyond flackery, even those who'd never said "nigger" on national TV.

The adventurous left was another matter. John Huey had had little contact with the people he'd pilloried for the last three years—he had to admit to having not a single left-of-center friend. But the ordeal of unemployment had altered his stereotype of the typical radical: gone was the bearded, hectoring gnome railing against VCR owners; replacing that weasel visage was a fetching and passionate Petra Kelly girl, a reader of Simone Weil, wearer of army-surplus pants, hot-blooded lover of John Huey Ketchum.

He kept his alluring apotheosis in mind and composed a letter to Jude Nelson, president of DC's principal left-wing think tank, The Institute of Critical Studies:

DEAR JUDE NELSON:

What the hell is a fascist like me doing writing a letter to you? Confessing, in a way, and asking for help.

You may know that for the last three years I've written a column for Solley News Service, and I've excoriated my share of leftists. I've been called "the bluntest Neanderthal stylist since Westbrook Pegler laid down his club"; I make no apologies for my past.

But something has happened on the Right, something ugly and profoundly threatening to this nation. The rugged individualist of American iconography is no longer a conservative hero. He (or she) has been replaced by the dandy, the smarty-pants, the jackanapes who scorns the common sense of ordinary people. The Right, once the guardian of the cherished frontier spirit, has become nasty and elitist. And I no longer want any part of it.

I've enclosed a couple of my columns. Though they are conservative in aim, I think you'll agree that mine is a populist vision that's really not very far from the populist Left. After all, how many "right-wingers" do you know who quote Huey Long? (My barnburner Grandaddy was a Long organizer.)

I've been thinking a lot about American politics lately, a lot about our antiquated Left-Right schematic. Frankly, I feel closer to the Left these days. I'd very much like to discuss my ideological sojourn with you; perhaps the Institute could use a hand who used to toil in the enemy camp. I'll call you next week.

Sincerely,
John Huey Ketchum

John Huey marched down to the post office and dropped the letter in the Local Mail bluebox, opening and reclosing the rectangular door three times to make sure his missive fell.

The Institute was domiciled in a McIntosh apple red townhouse, a block off DuPont Circle. A Rockwellian setting, sort of, if Norman had shaken his bucolic obsession and been more appreciative of urban bohemia. John Huey unlatched the waist-high black gate and bounded up the steps. A weatherbeaten bronze plaque read INSTITUTE OF CRITICAL STUDIES ESTABLISHED 1967 . . . AND JUSTICE FOR ALL. He walked in.

The receptionist, a dark-eyed hippie dream whose leonine curls tumbled down to the Viva Sandino! pin on her collar, buzzed Nelson using a communications system that looked straight out of a Wall Street brokerage or Hartford insurance mausoleum.

"He'll be right with you," she relayed, and before John Huey could browse through the Institute pamphlets that cluttered the lobby ("Working Toward Change in Guatemala," "Poisoned Milk for Third World Mothers?" "*New Jewel* Will Rise Again in Grenada"), Nelson was pumping his hand and leading him into a monkish office with bare walls. There was a small teak bookcase behind Nelson's chair. John Huey wanted to read the titles, but the only authors he could make out were Tom Paine and Tom Hayden. Who might have liked each other, he supposed, at least in 1963.

Jude Nelson's chair was no higher, or grander, or more thronelike, than John Huey's. That was unusual in PowerTown. He had a receding bush atop his head, a thin, probably asthmatic nose, and a tan sportcoat and unbuttoned blue shirt that revealed a shrubby clump of chest hair. A chain of some sort choked his neck, making him look like a lounge lizard who'd read Frantz Fanon.

"I'm familiar with your work, Mr. Ketchum, which is why I was shocked and surprised to get your letter," began Nelson, a whiff of pedantry convincing John Huey that Jude used to teach Soc 101 to braless coeds at U or State or Central before hopping aboard the thinkoisie gravy train.

Nelson fumbled in his suit pocket, withdrawing a pair of tortoiseshell glasses that he tacked on his face. He held John Huey's supplicating letter in his hands.

"West-brook Pegler," he said, splitting the first name in two. Nelson smiled to himself and kept reading. John Huey cleared his throat.

"Jack-anapes." This statement, too, defied reply.

"Hu-eee Long." Nelson read the letter as if it were divinely inspired, searching each word, each phrase, each syllable, for a meaning that John Huey knew wasn't there.

He removed his glasses when finished with the letter, dexterously pinwheeling them with his left hand while tapping an unheard syncopation with his right-hand knuckles upon his right kneecap. He was looking out his window at the Kronos Gyros shop across the street.

"I saw your performance on *Face the Nation* there a while ago," Nelson said to the pane of glass. "I wouldn't think our views are really compatible at all."

John Huey had written a mental speech for the occasion. He retrieved the outline in his mind and started his scripted discourse.

"I made a terrible mistake, Mr. Nelson [grimace for effect], one that I think implicates the whole conservative movement, not just me [swift double pivot]. You see, my grandpappy [practice had inured him to this mortifying homespunism], the Huey Long man, detested prejudice of any kind—class, race, whatever [sex would be a little much]—and he instilled that fierce egalitarianism in me. I was as shocked as anyone when that contemptible word spewed from my mouth [pristine victim/alien possession theme]. My grandpappy would've kicked the shit out of me if he was still alive [faint sympathy thrust]. For the longest time I wondered [evidence of reflective nature of the columnist], how could that word have sneaked into me and out of me? How, Lord, how? And then I saw it, clear as day—the grandpappy in me had been supplanted by the conservative-movement succubus. I'd forsaken my roots [return to admission of individual responsibility] and taken on foreign traits, at least on the surface [don't wanna sound like a pod-people paranoiac]. I won't name names [I'm no Elia Kazan], but I saw firsthand the racism that permeates the conservative establishment. I heard the word 'nigger' bandied about like an innocuous preposition: it stunned me at first [guileless farm boy corrupted by the city]. And it affected me, more I guess than I like to admit [hey, I'm bein' honest with ya]. I escaped, in a way, and have just rethought everything. As a result, I've returned to my roots. I've regained my social consciousness, in a way. [Smile as we wrap it up.] I have seen the enemy—at much closer range, I'd hazard, than most Institute scholars. I think I'd bring to the Institute a talented mind and pen, plus invaluable [once-in-a-lifetime offer!] experience on the other side. I'd like to write for the Institute, Mr. Nelson, and I do think you need me [close with a bit of career counselorism, just in case those get-a-job books are right]."

He settled back into his chair and waited for a response.

Nelson's stare hadn't moved from the plate glass picture window, through which he seemed to stare still at the gyro shop across the street. Who knew what that meant? Neither spoke for a good thirty seconds.

Finally Nelson swiveled back toward the intruding beggar squirming in the guest chair. He fastened his gaze about a foot over John Huey's head. John Huey wondered whether old Jude, too, might not have sneaked a peek or two at *Looking Out for #1.*

"Puttin' your ass through a Ringer," punned the imp in John Huey's head. When a smile threatened to twist our hero's lips, Nelson spoke up.

"Look, Mr. Ketchum. I asked you here today for one reason. Maybe it was noble, maybe not. I wanted to see a conservative crawl and beg."

A frisson of fear shot through John Huey's nerve network. "He's taping this!" It'd be a hot item on the pool-swimming, brie-snorting, sweater-tied-around-the-neck Georgetown lefty circuit.

"Mr. Ketchum," continued Nelson, whose eyes now met his interlocutor's, "you're not only a racist troglodyte. You're a liar, a hypocrite, a spineless hack who'd exploit his mother for a taste of fame and money. Get out of my office, get out of my Institute, go suck up to your fascist ex-colleagues if you want a job. You make me sick."

John Huey had no scripted response. His impulse was to spit at Nelson, to call him a sleazy, sybaritic Sandinista hypocrite, but just as there was no audience for Nelson's animadversions, so would there be no witnesses to a fine invective-laced retort. The only reason to fight was to defend some innate, unyielding sense of honor, a pride in self that was without vanity or posing.

John Huey stood up, eyes glued to the carpet, and walked out.

A chill fall wind was blowing dissevered newspapers down the sidewalk, this way and that. The *Post*'s fashion section flapped noisily at John Huey's ankles, like a barking paper dog. He tried to step over it, to no avail. An arctic fashion model bedizened in plutocratic jewels was nipping at his left shin, and she would not be shaken. It took him a minute or two to pry the fugitive sections off his lower torso; he stuffed them in a pale blue DC Is a Capital City box.

On the walk home, John Huey tried to work up a healthy hatred of Nelson. Humiliated by an arch-enemy! Faced by a flat-footed white boy! Stung by a treacherous and oily little insect!

But the hate was submerged by self-pity. All John Huey felt was tired and beaten and resigned. He had to leave DC: his shame here was complete, total, consummate. He knew his final destination.

6

At the National Press Club mall John Huey slouched in a red plastic chair, ass sliding downward so he had to lift his trunk up every minute or so. The mall was a festival of colors, aqua and pastel and cherry and an otherwordly turquoise that cupped the garbage bins.

Purposeful men strode past, mustard rimming their dry mouths; a Greek gesticulated, urgently, to an uncomprehending crone. Piped-in music—"All the leaves are brown/And the sky is gray"—competed for auricular attention with the hearty laughs of sweaty workmen. A queer, delicately brushing his thinning hair, swished by.

John Huey surrendered to the beer crashing in his brain, splashing, dampening every crevice, filling all his secret holes till, woozy, swaying, he began counting the studs on the black iron base of the adjacent table. The cruel, malicious laughter of idle rich boys, tanned, tank-topped, shook him from his reverie.

Ah, life. A fat woman, layers of pink flesh engorging her arms, waddled by. The college boys' repellent laughter amplified, louder, louder still, till it drowned the synthetic rock muzak, the earnest chitchat, the gentle remonstrances of young mothers strolling their babes. The fat woman was on fire! Flames: sleek, undulating rolls of fire engulfed her obese form. Sparks flew from her eye sockets, her breasts were ablaze, her arms, legs, thighs; he watched her feet burn, her face char, then in one brilliant flash it crumbled, thousands of embers drifting to the mall's white tile floor.

———

The sloped marble steps at the base of Daniel Webster's 16th Street statue were frigid to the touch, not unlike the Great Man himself. Nighttime, the dark cape overhanging the stubby midtown skyline. The Fall.

The slab of stone against which John Huey slumped bore the orator's epitaph: EXPOUNDER AND DEFENDER OF THE CONSTITUTION. John Huey unsheathed a felt-tipped pen and tried to engrave an addendum: OPPORTUNISTIC CROOK AND SHYSTER LAWYER. Which the Expounder and Defender was, though no one remembers.

The marble admitted no defacing.

Well-manicured shrubs rimmed Webster Circle. "Somebody must cut the fuckers two or three times a month," mused John Huey. He wondered how difficult a landscaping job would be to obtain, entertaining the thought of himself in grass-stained workclothes, carefully trimming the hedges beneath the lifeless gaze of Daniel Webster.

But he didn't think the DC government would hire a white guy. Especially him.

He spat at the ground—a thick globule of fresh saliva—and he watched it melt into the earth. He spit again, and again, four more times, fascinated by the simple process of decomposition. He had a brief Thoreau reverie—"I'll buy an empty lot on Horseshoe Road and be a cranky old Batavia hermit that kids make up stories about"—but he knew that escape was not expiation, seclusion not damnation.

Would he miss Washington?

John Huey tried to capture and muster the happiest moments of his domicile in the Nation's Capital: seeing his first column in print; talking girls with an oddly laconic Bertram; advising a Senate candidate from Wyoming who'd flown all the way across the country to meet with "opinion leaders" (who feigned omniscience and superciliously dismissed the outlander's genuinely bold ideas as "unrealistic and impractical"); the party at which a sloshed sexy intern told him "you are *soooo* attractive."

Was that it?

Were six years of his life (the prime twelfth!) nothing more than a jumble of disconnected moments, fleeting, transitory, illusory?

He wracked his brain for more, for *solidity*, for *coherence*, for *meaning*, palms thumping the cold marble as if to jump-start his memory.

He remembered: the party at the American Foundation at which a congressman told him, "I read you religiously"; gleefully tossing constituents' mail with Bertram in the dying days of their Senate careers; getting drunk at the Redskins–Dallas game and missing the overtime touchdown because he was vomiting into a urinal; pilfering a ghostwritten O'Rourke book manuscript and daring his craven newspaper friends to expose, using this incontrovertible source, the polymathic legislator as just another fake (they refused: the deception wasn't "news"); going to a White House reception and glimpsing the President, surrounded by the courtiers and courtesans of power (John Huey's friends).

There was no thread, no seamless silken strand, no deep reverberating chord that played throughout his adult life. It was a congeries of coincidences, he told himself, reaching for an alliterative phrase like the washed-up columnist he was. A heap of hopelessness, a pile of pathos.

He was leaving tomorrow. He didn't think he'd miss Washington.

Packing his sundry possessions into a khaki duffel bag and three suitcases was, at first, a remarkably unsentimental undertaking. Clotheswise, John Huey separated wheat from chaff and kept the latter.

Peeling Adidas, paint-splattered T-shirts, white socks, faded jeans stiffened by years of desuetude, anything flannel that didn't look L. L. Bean—keep.

Pinstriped Brooks Brothers suits (two), seersucker right-wing summer uniform, wing-tipped shoes, blue shirts costing more than $15, the unused Italian cologne Bertram always gave him at Christmas—toss.

At work, voluminous files whistled down the trash chute in a five-minute fit of manilorrhea: "Peace" Movement (ironic quote marks), Transportation, Goldwater '64, Stupid Liberal Quotes, Civil Wrongs, TV and Pop Culture, Foundation Grants, Solley Stuff, DC Government, Nicaragua Libre, South Africa, DemRusskies, Tree Huggers, Kennedys, Media Bias, Movie Politics, New Left, LesboFeminism, God Issues, Oil and Strategy—all were consigned to the sooty, rat-dwelling netherworld in the abyss of the trash chute.

John Huey saved just one file—Huey Long/Grandpa. He fit it in the side pocket of his shabbiest suitcase.

At home, he tossed away the pile of canceled checks, dead bills, sales flyers, and propaganda that filled two kitchen drawers. He'd examine each item for perhaps a millisecond, hear his heart/mind chorus boom "No," then flick the otiose nuisance into his yellow garbage pail.

"So long, life," he said melodramatically whenever a candidate's handbill or bumper sticker or appeal for cash was discarded.

John Huey's disposal routine was disrupted when his sorting produced an old black-and-white photo, KODAK stenciled on its reverse, just above the cryptic inscription MAY 68 NO JUNOIRS!

It was his mother's handwriting. No orthographer, she'd misspelled JUNIORS. The tad in the photo's foreground—

frail stripling, brush-cutted with little-boy vacation-gleam in his eye—was John Huey.

A muscular man, sweatshirted, Bermuda-shorted, butch-cutted, grinning a beatific paternal grin, stood several paces behind the boy. He had an unmemorable face, devoid of blemishes or striking features, yet to John Huey's adult eye a nimbus surrounded the man: a halo, yes, seared into the photographic paper, every bit as graven as the impression that Our Lord's angelic countenance has imprinted upon the Shroud of Turin.

The saint in the picture was John Huey's father.

NO JUNOIRS! was a wife's graceful reproach to a husband who saw himself as the boy's template. The husband's name was Richard Huey Ketchum.

Dad.

John Huey's eyes clouded. A monsoon of self-pity, disguised as shame, overswept him.

"I couldn't shine. . . ." John Huey began, till the bathetic triteness of the imminent remark froze his tongue. He saw his whole life as a sophisticated movie, one in which the commonplace remark was to be avoided and the maudlin sentiment mocked.

He wished he could let go.

"Oh, Dad," he mumbled, "I never sold you out, I never used you. And I could have. Can you forgive my wretched soul, let that one virtue outweigh my crimes?"

John Huey spoke the truth. The grave robbing he'd performed with such aplomb on Fred—Grandpappy, if you prefer—he never duplicated with Ketchum *père*. His forebear. His sire. His dad.

He hadn't visited his dad's grave since high school. (He'd never visited his grandad's.) Indeed, his father had long ceased to exist for John Huey even in spirit form. He felt no firm invisible hand steadying his shoulder in moments of duress, he heard no comforting whisper from the beyond, he did not walk emboldened in parlous days, inspirited by the miraculous presence of the departed. He knew that others experienced a knowledge, an awareness, a transgenerational harmony and unity with their predecessors. He was willing to believe in ghosts and wraiths and resurrections and Ouija boards. He was just waiting for evidence.

John Huey's mind becalmed as one, two, three beers coursed through his system. He remembered September 1971, not in narrative dream or chronological order but in a brief, overlapping, exaggerated reel of images. Like a movie, he thought, and indeed he wondered if the moiety of his recollections, rewound so often on his dilapidated spool, might be fantastic distortions of the truth.

He remembered his father walking smartly, with purpose always, in his gray guard uniform. There was a nameplate, a tiny American flag, and the ensign of New York State sewn to his shoulder—epaulets, yes. His father hated the Governor—"Millionaire prick don't pay us shit, wants us all in cages, niggers and guards too." A rare use of obscene language, at least in front of JUNOIR. Called home from school—was it a Thursday, that dread September morn?—

mother smothering her bewildered son, frantically tearful, neighbor Mrs. Valley peeling potatoes stupidly at sink, she's crying too, blurts out "Oh little Johnny, oh Little Johnny, they've got your daddy, ohohoh." Watching TV dumbly, phone interrupting every ten minutes or so, Mom hugs, entrusts her son to obese Mrs. Valley, runs to car and drives away, so slowly it seems—the Mustang crawls down Elm Street and Mrs. Valley is ringing up the whole town. "Oh God, oh merciful God, the inmates went crazy over at Attica They're holding the guards, they say one's dead already Oh God they'll kill them all, they took Dick, they took poor Dick, Carol drove over there but I don't know what she can do there that she can't do here, the prison's no place for a woman, oh I hate that prison, I hate it, I always knew something like this would happen, oh they'll kill them all, the animals will slit their throats every last one of them." Ominous TV pictures of Afroed black inmates saying Brother Brother, saying we're not afraid to die, we're already dead, blindfolded guard slumped at table in pathetic submission (did the white cloth soak up his tears?)—angry townsfolk whom big-city editing reduces to blabbering rural redneck idiots, wives sobbing hysterically, "I just want him to know I love him I love you dear If you can hear me in there I love you I'm waiting for you Everything will be all right." Staying home from school while Mom stays in Attica at Jamaski's house, she calls "Little John Huey you be a big boy you be a brave man your Daddy is in big trouble so you have to be the man of the house Can you do that for me hon?" "Yes Mommy" and he starts crying, confused about why the scary black men have captured Daddy, secretly thrilled that the news every night shows a map of the Eastern states with New York highlighted in off-yellow and a star in the western part with ATTICA in solid black letters—Fred splitting time between Attica vigil and tending/talking/walking through Blind School Park assuring "Don't worry Don't worry little John Huey, your Daddy will be all right"—Fred and Mr. Shedard and Mr. MacDougall and Mr. Kelly sitting around the kitchen table, drinking Genesee. MACDOUGALL: "That goddam bastard Rockefeller oughtta go in and clean those niggers up, blow 'em all to hell, free those poor guys." FRED (choking on his words): "Why, that rich jerk wouldn't know his ass from a hole in the ground. Damn millionaires and niggers takin' over this country, everything's for the rich, rich get this, rich get that, and whatever's left over they throw to the niggers, that rich jerk better protect those guards." SHEDARD: "I'd go in and kill the sons of bitches myself, then use whatever I got left on Rocky and the damn TV reporters, harassing everybody, makin' us look like the bad guys." KELLY: "Well, I'll tell ya, I think the guards'll get out peacefully, somehow, I don't know, but I think the one good thing that'll come out of all this is that Rocky can kiss his career goodbye." SHEDARD: "Amen."

On the fourth day Mommy comes home, her cheeks sunken like a lady vampire, saying "I gotta get some sleep, I just gotta get some sleep." She kisses John Huey's forehead, pats his light dusting of hair, says, "Oh, you've been such a good boy, such a good boy. Your Daddy would be proud of you, being the man of the house." Then she collapses into the marital bed, smothering her drawn face in Dick's pillow and crying, in fits and starts, until she falls asleep. Phone rings, Mrs. Valley answers, silence. "Oh, my God, Lord have mercy," she drops the phone, it hits a chair and dangles above the floor, suspended like an unwound yo-yo. She runs to the TV, turns it on, it takes a minute to warm up, hours it seems, and over a placid close-up of Attica's impregnable stone walls a voice is urgently reading. "To repeat, this morning at nine forty-five a team of New York State Troopers stormed the prison. Reporters heard the crack of arms fire, shouting, screaming, more gunfire, it lasted no more than twenty minutes; dozens of inmates are reported dead, as well as some guards." John Huey sits transfixed in front of the set all morning, imagining his father, the handsome hero, escaping his chains and fetters, outwitting his captors, stealing a gun and picking off the Afro hairdos one by one, clean shots splitting their skulls.

Fred walks in the door early evening, somber, funereal, eyes reddened as never before. "Come here, little John Huey," he says, and the boy, the awful truth dawning on him, runs to his grandfather and sobs into his chest, "Grandpa, Grandpa, did Daddy get killed?" Fred, gaining strength from the solace he's providing, rocks the boy as he once rocked another crewcut lad. "Yes, little John Huey, your daddy was killed, he was killed in the riot." Fred kisses the boy's pate. "Your mommy needs you to be strong. She's over at Attica, but she'll be home in a little while. Be a strong little man." Fred brushes the boy's hair for the longest time, as

Mrs. Valley busily phones the neighbors to tell them what they already know.

Richard Huey Ketchum received a full-honors, dress-blue New York State funeral in Batavia. St. Theresa's was packed to standing room with Dick's friends and family and guards and troopers and sympathetic strangers and government apparatchiks and the plain curious. An American flag draped the coffin. Mom, Grandpa, and John Huey sat in the front pew. John Huey marveled at the crowd, which far exceeded any gathering he'd experienced, especially in church. The diocesan bishop, making a rare foray out of Buffalo and into the sticks, said mass; he assured the mourners that Dick had passed on to a better life and was at that very moment sitting at the right hand of the Lord. The head warden of the New York State prison system delivered a clichéd, insincere address that scanted God but attested that Dick and the ten other dead guards were "true heroes" whose "sacrifice can never be forgotten" and whose widows and children "will be taken care of, rest assured."

Fred stared at the kneeler whenever the bishop or warden spoke too intimately of Dick; afterward he called them "crooks," "bums," "big-shot jerks," and "idiots."

The mass adjourned at 11:00 A.M., and as the family exited the church, they were met by a battery of cameras and reporters clutching microphones, mindful of the situation's delicacy but ludicrously hoping that the bereaved might throw an impromptu press conference. Before the mass, Mrs. Valley suggested to John Huey that he "salute your daddy's casket when they carry it out of the church, just like little John-John Kennedy." He agreed, having not the slightest idea who this John-John was, and he intended to snap off a cute tad salute, until Fred, who'd overheard the instructions, took John Huey aside and told him, "Don't pay any attention to what Mrs. Valley says, she's nice but an old fool." He skipped the salute.

That night, John Huey and his mom watched themselves on national TV: the camera revealed a grief-stricken, black-veiled widow stepping into a waiting funeral-home limousine with an irascible elderly man and a confused boy wearing his best (and only) suit and a crooked clip-on tie. The anchorman prefaced the troika's appearance with the observation that "the residents of the small and sleepy village of Attica, New York, stunned and confused by the events that have made their hamlet the center of the world's attention, started burying their dead today."

John Huey and his mother watched the procession without comment. Never did they mention their TV debut, until fifteen years later Mom said, "I wish they had VCRs back then. I would have taped your father's funeral and the reports."

He couldn't tell if she was serious or, in a departure from character, joking. When her son left home for college, Carol Ketchum married another guard—he'd retired shortly after the riot—and the couple left Western New York immediately, migrating to Florida to escape the winters and the prison.

John Huey regarded her remarriage as a betrayal of his father, and he suspected the newlyweds of cuckolding Dick in the last days of his life.

For her part, Mom exulted at the chance to start anew. Her life after Dick's death and before John Huey's maturity was dreary and monotonous. She resented the pity the townspeople felt toward her, and even more she hated the idea of living out her life in thrall to a ghost, to a vanished piece of her past. She leaped at the opportunity to remarry, and she didn't mind the separation from her son, so long as they remained on cordial terms and talked monthly on the telephone.

Their long-distance conversations were pleasantry-exchanges of the most prosaic sort.

"Hi, Mom."

"Hi, Johnny, how are you?"

"Oh, not too bad. How 'bout you?"

"Good, good."

"How's Henry?"

"Fine, Henry's fine."

And so on.

Her crack about the VCR, dropped into a discussion of Christmas presents, was the sole reference to Dick that either had ever let slip into their meaningless dialogues.

Unlike many Attica families, Mom and Son Ketchum seemed remarkably unobsessed with the events of September 1971. Neither read any of the didactic postriot books (no Attican ever wrote one, oddly). John Huey thumbed through Tom Wicker's *A Time to Die* once in a bookstore, but Wicker's snide references to "the drudge life in Alexander, New York," and "watching cheerful Batavians enjoying themselves at the local hot-spot," *i.e.* "a bowling-alley restaurant," offended the bereaved as so much upper-class Manhattan spittle on modest upstate gravestones.

The Ketchum survivors ignored the occasional commemorations and hostage-family get-togethers held over the years. A 1983 newspaper article piqued John Huey's curiosity—the reporter claimed that nearly all the slain guards died wearing inmate uniforms—but there was really no point in dredging up sunken memories, was there?

7

Excerpts From John Huey's Journal

To Batavia, to Attica, to the Genesee Country.

To a forgotten hinterland, forlorn and powerless, a crumbled idol of Jeffersonian America.

To a province, really, a captive nation, helpless and supine under the velvet boot of the capital.

In the once-rich loam of Genesee I shall find my professional grave, in a cemetery abundant with arrowheads and rusty farm implements and chalky ancestors and human dross that would sicken Edgar Lee Masters.

For, brethren, I have sinned, and for my sins—those

multiple black indelibles crisscrossing my soul—I am cast out of my tribe of choice, back to the tribe of my birth.

I haven't a single living relative in that godforsaken cowpatch, that benighted, inbred pool of ignorant hicks and philandering Rotarians. Buried in the asshole of the world, Batavia is a dying town, a sick valetudinarian forever whining about the foggy halcyon days of noble Injuns and hardy settlers and stout pioneer women and virtuous founding fathers to whom collapsing statues were erected long, long ago. Ah, magnificent and storied past!

Never mind that the noble Seneca's great-great-grandsons breathe cheap liquor while their great-great-granddaughters make ten bucks a throw as fuck machines at biker bars adjoining the Tonawanda Reservation. Never mind the swindling, venal character of Batavia's earliest magistrates or the gluttony and incompetence of today's boozy, lecherous public servants. Never mind the abandoned plants and the pathetic Chamber of Commerce efforts to recapture the fleeing capitalists. ("Genesee Community College can make Batavia the Silicon Valley of Western New York!") Never mind, indeed, that revisionists have pegged Robert Morris, the Declaration-signing Father of Batavia, as a corrupt, swinish land speculator.

The historians call this the "Burned–Over District," for once upon a time its soil begat abolitionists and suffragettes and the Angel Moroni and Shakers and Perfectionists and incendiary revivalists and, best of all, Batavia's sole contribution to national political discourse, the glorious Anti–Masonic Party. The land west of Syracuse and east of Buffalo coursed a "psychic highway," in gentle poet Carl Carmer's words, and the pyrotechnics of all these cornfed seers and saints and mad visionaries scorched the earth so thoroughly that nothing has grown there for the last hundred years. Save me.

I escaped at age eighteen, minimizing, I prayed to God (yes! I used to do that) the provincial damage wrought upon my being. I returned to see my Grandpa Fred once or twice a year, usually at Christmas, nimbly avoiding my polygamous Florida-bound mom, but for all practical purposes I'd fully extirpated the Batavia poison and fully expatriated myself by age twenty-five. I suppose any number of my dull classmates have vaguely followed my pilgrim's progress (I heard the *Batavia Daily View* once ran a brief item on me), but I've kept in touch with no one, a perfect divorce. With the Washington, D.C. emetic, I purged my toxic birthright.

My return, therefore, vitiates my entire adult life. Every step I took away from the Burned–Over mausoleum has been for nought. The path I traversed turned out to be a circle; the sum of my professional accomplishments, which I once thought considerable, is irredeemably, irrefragably, irreducibly, zero.

Ah, mortification. To see the acne-scarred faces of my boyhood chums scrutinize my ragged form. To hear the waspish voices of malicious gossips whispering tales of my turpitude and demise. To feel the lash of Genesee County's disapproval sting my naked back. To speak of my shame to any who ask; to abase myself in the most spectacularly mundane fashion; to surrender physically what I have already lost professionally, spiritually, emotionally. To die in Batavia, a second time, with no hope for rebirth.

Country roads, take me home.

―――

My back-of-the-bus deep sleep was interrupted by the unmistakable tubercular hacking cough of a Leeper, the Genesee County Kennedys of petty theft and drunk driving and intrafamily fistfighting quarrels and unwed pubescent mothers losing rotted teeth, yesterday, today, and tomorrow, as an unbroken Leeper circle makes the bloody transit from beery womb to earthly immurement. No Zonta Club or National Honor Society for this brood.

I awoke to see the final miles of Route 5 gloomily parade before my bus window:

We glide through the hamlets, the bargetowns that died aborning, the trading posts where supply exceeded demand;

Mounds, clumps, pyramids of gravel lie in wait;

Anxious to displace the grass and rocks and decapitated corn stalks, the nasty little shrubs and weeds and hardscrabble ground, rendered inarable by greed and neglect;

We have always the road, paved soil, conveying the natives (for immigration is one way here) across flat farmland, straight for the most part until a serpentine curve catches the driver unawares;

Trees, lucky to escape the highwayman's bulldozer, line the road in mute reproach, relics of Iroquois days;

Ersatz trees, telephone poles—linked, omnipresent, spaced regular as rain;

A silo stands in the distance;

Mobile home parks beckon to Burned–Over dropouts, "Come, my wretched sons, live in me, love in me, fuck in me, fight in me, die in me," and the unsentimental heed the call;

Barbed wire rusted past dullness incarcerates an empty red barn;

The Stafford Drive–In is playing R-rated stewardess movies;

Lazily, the Tonawanda Creek meanders into sight, offering its salty carp to the angling niggers;

Black-man shanties, tucked underneath the Route 5 promontory, are fragrant with frying fish;

Speed-limit signs, hammered into the incinerated earth, remind the locals that Babylon rules;

In the vastitude of pine and dirt and harvested corn, yesterday's boys drink at Mickey's, Stoney's, the Dewdrop Inn;

An insensate Indian snores on the pinball table;

He will sleep tonight under the yellow bunting proclaiming Lou Bradshaw's Oldsmobile;

Amidst the splendid decay of arcadian America, with

its collapsing barns, untended land, fallow fields, defiled glens, and abandoned small shops;

After a stretch, the road catches up with the Creek again, a barechested boy floats languidly on a wooden raft, lost in the daydreams of rural boys everywhere;

When he comes home at sunset his mother will ask him what he did all day, and he will say, "Nuthin'";

I can see the Batavia watertower;

Town Line Road escorts us home, her verges consecrated by car dealerships and new discount stores;

A handful of Founders' homes survive, Gothic monuments to simpler days;

(You should see the House of the First Dentist!);

1820s stone dwellings built by Ethans and Edwards and Josiahs . . . gone forever;

The Tomilson mansion, gray and foreboding, breathes exhaust from revving Camaro engines in the Bob's Big Boy parking lot;

Spires and steeples and hard white churches exact Methodist virtue, offering $150 Bingo jackpots;

The beige monolithic Golden Age Towers imprisons the elderly;

While the young age apace in the horrific Genesee Valley Mall, desecratory eyesore squatting over ancient Batavia's burial ground;

As the bus pulls into the terminal, I read puzzled old Edmund Wilson: "I come to feel, when I have been here for any length of time, the *limited* character of upstate

New York. It does not go back very far into the past and it does not come very far forward into the present";

My feet touch Batavia pavement, and I remember why I left.

———

"A prophet will always be held in honor, except in his hometown."

Spent my first sidereal day draining a bottle of DeKuyper and a six-pack of Genny Cream Ale; spent the second floor-stricken with throbbing prickly tumor stuck in my head and a thousand balls of yarn stuffed in my eyes, *i.e.* dust in my contacts. Went down to Melia's newsstand, asked for a *Washington Post*; met with a quizzical shrug by a muscle-shirted boy at counter. Noticed a stack of *Times*es piled high, unmolested, while courteous line of customers bought lottery ticket after lottery ticket, many pausing at the door to scratch their cards, the luckiest returning to queue to claim their One Free Ticket prizes. Didn't know panem et circenses could be played solitaire.

Writhing on the floor of Room 16 of the YES VACANCY Batavia Motor Hotel, suing for peace with the oncological killer inside me, I tried to compose a prose ode to my abode, in the manner of Russell Kirk's vaporous eclogues to Mecosta. But I have no Piety Hill; I resolved to find (or fabricate) one tomorrow.

The third day the headache disappeared (it *migrainted*, hahaha), and I wrapped myself in my army-surplus jacket and walked. I walked, enshrouded, down ghostly Main Street. The brick barbershops and Woolworth's and Grant's and the Italian bars that the bad men used to stumble out of—they kidnapped children, so the story went—all those musty, primeval stores of my youth were gone, razed, demolished by the developer's ball in the urban renewal orgy of the American dotage. A mall, a single pentagonal enclosure guarded by a vast sea of pavement, stood upon Batavia's commercial graveyard. A marquee dominated the main entrance; the cineplex was showing three recent films, all starring attractive women who shimmy their luscious asses on private Malibu beaches all the livelong day. What do they think of the stolid, slothful, greasy, upright, ugly Batavians who sit in dark minitheaters watching their implausible charades?

Probably not much.

I walked past the firehouse, its seven shiny red engines and thirty-some firemen ("blazebusters" the *Batavia Daily View* calls them in venturesome reportorial moments) in a state of dubious vigilance, barely ready to smother the two big fires and countless smoky kitchens that menace the citizenry each year.

I walked past Mungo's Records, the tiny center of Genesee County hippiedom, memorialized when a 1969 sheriff's raid uncovered several pipes and a bag of marijuana seeds and the *Daily* plastered its front page:

"Hippies Nabbed in Undercover Dope Raid." I remember as a teen hating Mungo's: leather-jacketed, straggly-haired *cool ones* were always congregated at the entrance, blaring Boston and Styx and Black Oak Arkansas and swapping stereo tips. I got up the nerve once to ask for a Velvet Underground LP, and all chatter ceased. Mungo stroked his half-assed goatee, quipped, "I think you want the classical music store or sumptin'," and the rowdies erupted, their imbecile, I-oughta-kick-your-faggot-ass laughs chasing me out of the store, never to return.

I walked past the Benevolent and Protective Order of Elk Lodge 29 Batavia New York, up which steps I'd skipped the day Grandpa took me to vote with him. "C'mon, John Huey, come vote with me. Someday you'll have to do this, choose one crook over the rest, one rich bastard over the next. It's good for you to learn now how to do this." I remember a long hall with black-and-white photos of dead Elk, leading into a gymnasium of sorts, where dour white-haired ladies sat at three adjoining cardtables checking the credentials of prospective voters with all the gravity of a Calvinist minister inspecting miniskirted new parishioners. Grandpa, hand gently cupping my shoulder, led me to the booth, drew the curtain behind us, and studied the ballot. "Goddam Rockefeller," he mumbled, "I wouldn't vote for that millionaire if he put a gun to my head." Reading on down the ballot, "That guy's a nigger-lover," he said of some Senate candidate, pressing his opponent's lever. "I can't stand that bastard," he declared of the Attorney General, and when he determined that the Republican and Democratic candidates for Comptroller were both Jews, he voted Socialist Workers. All of the candidates for local office had slighted him at one time or another, and those that hadn't were "too cocky," or "rich bastards," or "just no damn good." Grandpa abstained from those races. We left the booth and the Elks club, my heart pitterpattering, thrilled at my secret act of voting. (Fred let me cast the Socialist Workers vote, since the party was stuck at ballot's bottom, reachable by an eight-year-old's hand.) "They're no good, none of 'em," he told me as we trudged through the snow. "Not a one of 'em cares about the people, unh uh, no how. You just remember that." I don't think Fred ever voted again.

I walked past Linda Hunnage's house, a jerrybuilt one-story plywood rectangle, her tiny yard abloom with weedy foliage. A lone purplish vine snaked up the eavestrough, indifferent to the brick that had been placed across its stem to choke its growth. (Why hadn't the unruly weed just been chopped off?) Linda Hunnage was the white-trash quintessence, a sloe-eyed Appalachian transplant who lagged in first grade, straggled in second, stumbled in third, and freefell in the fourth, after which she vanished into the retard class morass. I remember fourth grade, Valentine's Day, the students dropping cards and candies into handmade mail pouches attached to each desk. Allowing for the odd rivalry or temporary split, the pouches filled equally with greetings, and the most ornate messages (BE MINE/ALL THE TIME/VALENTINE) were deposited multiple times in the prettiest girls' receptacles. At the end of the half-hour allotted for delivering the valentines, I sat back down, pleased at my overflowing pouch. Linda Hunnage, I noticed, sat dolefully at her desk, staring at the two or three courteous, antieffusive missives she'd received. Loudly, I asked my neighbor for a card, scrawled *Unhappy V-Day HunHag* on it, let several giggling classmates in on my jest, and marched it over to the lonely little girl, barking, "Here, I forgot to give this to you." As I returned to my seat, asshole smirk smeared across my face, she ripped open the envelope eagerly and read my punning salutation. When I next looked, her head lay on her desk, and she was crying. Seeing the moisture glisten off her preternaturally white arm is the last memory I have of Linda Hunnage. Standing in front of her house, two decades later, after my fall, I wanted to knock on her door, see the light of recognition in her eyes, and drop to my knees, begging her for forgiveness, asking her to chastise me and smite me and maybe even fuck me. I wanted her wrath, her pure undiluted wrath-borne-of-childhood-cruelty, to lacerate me as I stood, naked and penitent. Alas, I couldn't even work up the nerve to peek in the window.

I walked past John Kennedy Elementary School, my alma mater. (Named, incredibly, for the district's first school superintendent.) I remember the charmless, gawky Robert Mount, a malnourished little eight-year-old monkey who'd flunked the first grade twice. Robert lived on the interminable Pratt Road, at the trailer-park end of the famous cross-county highway. His father, LaVerne, was always turning up on page eight of the *Daily*: "Pratt Road Man Arrested in Check Forgery," that sort of thing. A ne'er-do-well without a hint of roguish Puck—a loser. Mrs. Mount, as best I knew, was an enormously fat woman who shunned all PTA meetings and parent-teacher conferences and, the rumor went, beat Robert and his siblings with a spiked board. (The second-worst punishment in Batavia—undisputed champ was Churchill Tubbs's spooky Jamaican father, who shaved his boy's head and soaked it in orange juice. "That's the most terrible thing you can do to a colored guy," Michael Flynn informed me.) Robert Mount worshipped me, in a second grader's kind of way, and I was so pleased by his fawning that my initial fear of this bug-eyed, wiry classmate with the fetid scent quickly gave way to friendship. I went out of my way to include Robert in my clique, and I even forbore from the opportunity to drill his pathetic target in dodgeball. Robert, thrilled at making his first friend, gave me pencils, erasers, even a Monkees record he stole from his sister. (I gave it back.) When my birthday rolled around in December, I requested the customary party: all the boys in my class invited to a Saturday afternoon of cake, ice cream, dropping clothespins in a milk bottle, etc. My mother gladly assented, and she inscribed invitations that I was to deliver to my male sidekicks. I counted the letters; I came up one short. A minute's inspection revealed that Robert Mount's name was missing. I told mom. "Yes," she responded, "you have enough people on that list." "What difference would one more make?" I pressed. She offered one lame excuse, then another, till her patience vanished and truth won out. "Little John Huey, that Mount boy is no good. His family is trash. I don't want him in this house. Period." My household did not exalt what is now called "dialogue," so the matter was finished. I delivered the invites the next morning, as furtively as I could, but by lunch the party was topping the conversational agenda. Robert approached me, timidly, as he would a teacher, and said simply, "John Huey, why didn't you ask me to go to your birthday party?" I think his eyes welled with tears; I'm not sure, because I hastily mumbled an unconvincing "not enough room" and squirted away. Robert never talked to me again. He never talked to anyone, really, and when he died in a car crash at age sixteen everybody in high school feigned sadness and grief, mostly in an unsuccessful effort to get a day off. "A week of mourning for the unknown road kill," one wit declared.

The noonday church bells chimed, and I realized, with mounting dismay, that investing an unexceptional upbringing with myth and resonance was a task far beyond one born into the sodden embers of the Burned–Over District.

I walked past St. Theresa's cemetery, the venerable family boneyard. Surrendering to the maudlin impulse, I wondered if they'd bury me there. I wondered if anyone would come to my funeral. How unholy the priest's words would ring: "Dearly beloved, we are gathered here today to lament the passing of a man who rejected, then ignored, then exploited, his past. And the irony is, that past is scarcely more virtuous than his abominable adulthood! Rot in hell, wayward traveler." While imagining my send-off to perdition, I saw a funeral ceremony in the vicinity of the caretaker's house. My line of sight was obstructed by the Dean Richmond sepulcher, but I could make out seven vertical motionless bodies, collective eyes cast downward. No one moved for the longest while, till it seemed that one sleepy moment coextended with eternity. The sky was a soft, enveloping blue, and I wished that the body being so lovingly interred on this idyllic day was mine, and that my sullied soul could trade places with the heaven-bound spirit of the deceased. The gathering finally broke up, the seven eulogizers reluctantly dispersing to assorted cars parked along the well-trod path, and I surveyed the rows of untended graves, weeds cropping the stones.

I walked past the National Guard Armory, where as a teenager I played flying-elbow street hockey every winter Friday night. The twenty assembled goalies, wings, centers, defensemen, and scrubs played with unsportsmanlike cutthroat zeal, taking illegal slap shots and whacking at smaller opponent's ankles. I remember scoring a critical goal directly off a face-off: the red plastic blade of my stick meeting the hard rubber ball as it rebounded from the drop, my shot *whoosh* catching the upper right-hand corner of the net, much to the crouched goalie's surprise. I coasted on adrenalinergy the rest of the game, and in that magical hour I felt for the only time in my life the naturally fluid, effortless grace of the capable athlete. I ran home, skipping *wheeee* every few steps, and the merciless truth of the Armory Street Hockey League—that it consisted of shy, dateless boys who had nothing else to do on Friday nights—disappeared for one enchanted evening.

I walked past Dwyer Stadium, home of the Class-A Batavia Trojans, knights errant of my youth. I remember Jim Wosman's prodigious homeruns—lore has it that he hit one five hundred feet one night, all the way into the tennis courts, where he bopped some hapless girl on the head. I remember Tom Breving, the weak-hitting ambidextrous outfielder who used to yell, "You comin' to the game tonight, buddy?" when he saw me watching him mosey down Bank Street. I remember Richie Hills, the flamboyant, error-prone colored shortstop whose girlfriend sat behind the dugout and sang, in rich melodic lilt, "Come-*own* Rit-chie Hills!" whenever her man came to bat. I remember Brian Lane, the tobacco-spitting Alabama greyhound who stole home one night in the bottom of the ninth and turned every Little Leaguer in Batavia into a head-first slider. I remember manager Bob "Reb" Dustinger, chaw bulging from his cheek as he hurled a rackful of bats onto the infield, one at a time, javelin-style, until the owner dragged Reb's ejected ass into the clubhouse. (The umps needed police protection to leave Dwyer that night.) And I remember Dave Pike, gentle giant, the quiet, handsome catcher who was booted one night after arguing a balls-and-strikes call (my ears refused to hear his "What the fuck?!"). Lo and behold, fifteen minutes later Dave appeared, in street clothes, at our side in the grandstand. "Mind if I watch the game with you guys?" he asked, as if a crew of nine-year-olds were bigshots with lots better things to do than sit with the Trojans' slugging catcher. I can't recall what Pike and our gang discussed, but I do remember him buying us pop and hot dogs and getting the hugest kick out of our evaluations of his teammates. The grandstand is small, so everyone saw us, and when they walked by they'd all yell, "Hey, Dave, how much they payin' that ump?" and other standard baseball greetings, and Dave would smile and wave, and we'd lap it all up, every second of it, just us guys, Dave Pike's personal friends.

I walked past the Clansman (yes, its real name), the entertainmentless lounge where I drank my first bar booze. I was sixteen, nervous as hell, and halfway down the red-carpeted staircase I wanted to turn back, but my buddy Chuck Raffalo wouldn't let me. "Jeezus Christ, don't be a pussy. I been here before just act cool like you belong maybe we'll even pick up some chicks." I ordered a whiskey sour, my mom's favorite drink, and the amused mock-gruff wop bartender mixed the cocktail and said, "You be careful with this, pardner, it's got a kick that'll put hair on your balls," and everybody laughed, Chuckie too, and to escape the derision I said, "Let's go play some pool," and as I dismounted my stool I spilled the whiskey sour on Chuckie and they all laughed some more, and the bartender said, "Better cut him off, we don't want him to be too drunk for his date with Rosie Palm and her four sisters tonight," and I beat a swift retreat to a cacophony of ridicule.

I walked past Dr. Lee Noonan's erstwhile residence, the hub of Batavia's periodontal activity. Noonan was an absurd, princely jackass: towering six and a half feet tall, he wore a Moe Howard toupee and a pair of tassled alligator shoes whose price ($400) and place of purchase ("Toronto, Canada") he never tired of quoting. Noonan's imperious gumside demeanor and haughty airs (he never initiated a "hi," and he acknowledged the greetings of those he considered his social inferiors with an imperceptible nod) earned him his detractors, none so harsh as my Grandpa Fred. "Goddam tooth doctor," Fred groused one day as Noonan jogged by. "Thinks he's better'n the rest of us just 'cause he makes all kinds of money playin' around with your mouth, which is a part of the body that everyone has to keep healthy. Guys like that jerk Noonan are the ones Huey was against." Almost never did he call forth Huey in his excoriations; that invocation taught me that Grandpa hated Noonan with especial ardor. I got a call from Fred one Thursday afternoon in DC. "Hi, Grandpa, what's up?" I demanded. "I won't keep you long, John Huey," Fred assured me, "I just want to read you what's on the front page of the *Daily:* 'Batavia Doctor Arrested in Insurance Scam. By Jim Magell. (He mispronounced the last name, stubbornly, bull-headedly, knowing full well that the Magell family stressed the first syllable.) New York State police arrested Dr. Lee Noonan, 57, of Batavia, yesterday, charging him with filing fraudulent insurance claims totaling more than $400,000 over a nine-year period.'" He continued reading, voice resonant with elated vindication, and when he finished the seven-paragraph story, I said "Serves that crook right, huh, Grandpa?" and over the five-hundred-mile wire I heard a callused hand slap a shaky knee and an American voice say, "Yes, it sure does, heh heh, serves that cocky rich bastard right. I never liked that guy." I tried to sound hurried over the phone, and I guess I succeeded, because Fred said, "Well, I don't want to keep you, John Huey. You probably have more important things to do. Are you coming home soon?" He always asked me that question, and I replied, as always, "Uh, yeah, maybe, as soon as I can, Grandpa." "Good," he said. "Come home, and we can go visit Big Lee in Attica, heh heh." I grunted, prepared to hang up, and he concluded, "Rich guy like that jerk, he won't do time in prison, nohow. If some nigger stole four hundred thousand, why, they'd burn him in the electric chair, but Dr. Lee, oh no, he's Lee, he's a doctor, he's important, we can't put him in prison, he's no nigger, he's a rich mouth doctor. Why. . . ." I told Fred I agreed a hundred percent and we said good-bye. I went back to work, and I suppose he sat at the kitchen table, sipping black coffee and enjoying the hell out of that paper.

I walked past all that remained of the Batavia of my boyhood, past the fine modest homes and the ugly arriviste temples and the smattering of neighborhood businesses that had escaped Lou Montello's wrecking ball. The town seemed restful, content . . . inviting.

Was I really home?

I contemplated Batavia's placidity; I breathed with increasing pleasure its clean, unpolluted air. I saw a shooting star flash across the crepuscular sky, its trailings disappearing into the dark blue heavens. The glint of the meteorite led my eye to the eastern horizon, where I beheld an eerie and jarring prospect that reminded me where I was, and why I was here.

Looking homeward, I saw the Genesee Valley Mall.

8

After a week spent in hazy reminiscence and morbid speculation, John Huey moved out of the Batavia Motor Hotel and into a two-room apartment in Oak Creek Village, whose pastoral name the locals ignored, preferring the lovingly pejorative "Cardboard City."

Cardboard City was Batavia's first and only public housing project, a shabby, haphazardly spaced mess of two hundred ramshackle apartments with peeling white paint and perennially barren yards. It was built in the early '70s, when it served as a magnet for dozens of black Buffalo families seeking an escape from the forbidding city.

Once exposed to the harsh clime and chauvinism of Batavia, most of the black exiles repatriated themselves to the old neighborhoods, and Cardboard City became haven for the indigenous white trash. Her snaking roads, speckled with speedbumps, paralleled a cracked sidewalk replete with racing Big Wheels, used baby carriages pushed by homely unwed mothers, raucous urchins throwing bombs with deflated footballs, and a herd of wandering unsupervised three-year-olds with ice-cream-smudged mouths and dirty-smelly T-shirts.

John Huey moved his sleeping bag, dictionary, and transistor radio into Apartment 132, smack dab in the village's center. He moved in his meager possessions under cover of night, shamefacedly, humiliated not by his surroundings ("the elegant's graveyard," whispered the imp) but by the hint of permanence the move implied. He had been in Batavia seven days, and he was not dead. No crowning rebuke from his humble birthplace had been delivered; not a single soul had so much as recognized him. Though John Huey had never laid definite suicide plans, he was unprepared for the continuance of his life. (He had, thank God, taken $4,000 out of his DC bank—why let the state seize it?—so the specter of work needn't yet rear its ugly head.)

The flight to Batavia just all seemed so . . . pointless. He had no boyhood scores to settle, no reconciliation to effect, no scaled-down goals to meet, just . . . plain old living. He'd assumed that transplanting himself from DC to Batavia would be equivalent to tossing a fish onto the shore. The poor fish doesn't have to slit its gills or anything—it just flops around a bit, gives up the ghost, and dies. Properly functioning lungs and heart, he knew, could condemn a man to a long, healthy life.

John Huey's aquatic ruminations were disturbed by the tinny pop of a frying pan hitting the sidewalk. He looked out his window and saw a hefty, well-built thirtyish man bolt from a nearby apartment, followed by a shrieking blonde woman hollering, "Don't you walk out on me again, don't do this again Ronnie you son of a bitch, don't you walk out on your wife and baby, come back here you motherfucking son of a bitch."

The man kept walking, in crisp, compact strides, a perfect economy of movement—must've been a halfback, thought John Huey—until he reached the frying pan, which he picked up by the handle and flung—must've had a wicked fastball, too—at his trailing wife, who ducked just in time. The frying pan clanged off the screen door frame, and as the athlete drove away in his Dodge a waifish little girl in hand-me-down pajamas came running from the house and jumped into the blonde woman's arms. They rocked in melancholy rhythm.

Once the muscular pan-thrower vanished into the Cardboard City night, a benevolent afflatus pushed John Huey out his door to check on his neighbors' welfare. They did not notice his approach.

"Hi," he said, "my name's John Huey, and I saw what happened. I live in one thirty-two. Are you guys OK?"

The mother pivoted to address the cowardly samaritan, daughter clinging to her bosom. "Yeah. Thanks. That was just my husband. He's an asshole."

Never had John Huey seen a more ensnarled head of hair.

A clump of straw here, a thatch there, long smooth tresses that ended abruptly in Gordian knots: how on earth did she comb that rat's nest? The moonless sky obscured her face; she seemed prematurely wrinkled, the kind of chain-smoking slut whom nice college-bound boys beat off to at sixteen, pass over at twenty-six, pity at thirty-six.

The little girl made no impression on him. Cute, with her mom's sandy locks, probably traumatized by Attila the Father.

The colloquy stalled—John Huey hadn't a clue what he should say to a typical denizen of the *Daily View*'s Page Eight. "Uh, I gotta be getting back to my place. I left the radio on," he said enigmatically. "If you need anything, anything at all, just knock. I'm in one thirty-two."

The woman set her daughter down. "Thanks, really. My name's Wanda, and this is my daughter, Dominique. 'Nique, say hi to . . . what'd you say your name was?"

"John Huey."

"John Huey. That's a funny name, if you don't mind me sayin' so."

"I don't mind," he said honestly, thankful that the word jam had been broken. "I guess it's a weird name, at least the Huey part."

"You from here?"

He hesitated. He'd forgotten to construct a fictive résumé.

"Uh, yeah, sort of. Lived in Washington, now I live here, for a little while anyway."

That oughta keep her guessing, he thought. Gives me an extraterrestrial aura.

"Hmmmm," she responded, not obviously intrigued. "Well, listen, why don't you stop by tomorrow. I get lonely for company around here. Do you work?"

"Uh, no, not here I don't." (Shit, he panicked—is she thinking that I'm an unemployed Batavia lunk filling out busboy applications?)

"Good. Then stop by. I'm home all day tomorrow. It's my day off. Well, 'bye."

And with that Wanda, Dominique in tow, returned whence she came, leaving the frying pan to gather bugs in the tall grass next to her porch.

He accepted her invitation.

Wanda welcomed him into her apartment; his perfunctory "nice place you got here" rang deafeningly hollow in the disheveled, unvacuumed sty.

"Want a beer or a glass of pop?" she asked as she dampened a cloth and daubed a bluish bruise whose locus was her left eyebrow.

"Yeah, I'll have a brew if you don't mind," he said.

He avoided looking at the eye welt so studiously that she felt compelled to explain.

"It was a nigger boy on a bike that done it."

Wanda put an ice-packed towel over her left eye. The fading riffs of *Entertainment Tonight* floated from the bedroom TV into the living room. John Huey wondered if the TV in this house had an Off switch. The screech of the screen door slamming shut interrupted his speculations.

"Wanda goddammit where in the fuck am I s'posed to park with 'Nique's goddam Big Wheel takin' up my space?"

Ronnie, partner in last night's frying pan toss, was home. Ruler of this hearth.

"Uh, honey, she just. . . ."

"The fuckin' transmission's shot again, as if I didn't know who. . . ."

He trailed off, point made, daring her to venture a protest. Ronnie brushed by Wanda's visitor, his beefy upper body tautened, proud, as if a decade and a half had melted and he was back in a dingy high-school locker room, shaking down mama's boys and smart kids for dollar bills.

He stood silently over Wanda, glaring, till she opened her mouth. At which point he yelled.

"Why don't you watch that kid? Your supervision, she's probably playin' with niggers every day. 'Nique's gonna be gettin' raped or fucked by that little nigger across the street if you don't watch out."

No matter how loudly Ronnie screamed, how blasphemous his scoldings, or how near violence he came, the brute never moved a muscle without cause. No gesturing, no hand-waving, not even a roll of the head. Ronnie appeared unable to vent the ugly maelstrom inside, all those swelling black waves of hatred and fury that swirled through his innards. Not one crummy droplet of sweat squeezed out his pores. Ronnie resembled, to John Huey anyway, a volcano, with all the tranquility of Krakatoa two minutes before eruption.

Now Ronnie was in the kitchen, rummaging through the

refrigerator. The crayon drawings of Mommy and Daddy did not pacify him.

"Nothing in this goddam house to eat!" he roared, strangely accenting the last word.

He pulled a red carton of milk from the top shelf, popped the flap, and drained an entire quart straight from the cardboard, the way assholes always do.

John Huey stood, ashamed of his awkwardness. "Well," he started, "I better be going. I'll come back some better time."

Ronnie ignored him.

As John Huey walked to the door, he resolved to say *something* in defense of his hostess.

"Look, Ronnie, aren't you a little curious about your wife's black eye? It wasn't there when I saw her last night."

Ronnie transfixed his guest with lifeless blue eyes. (Did they sparkle when his mom held his tiny hand on the first day of school?) He ran his right hand through his longish, knotty mane of black hair, then battened his inanimate gaze on Wanda.

"So, whuh happened to your eye?" he finally asked.

She paused, bit her lip, tugged at her Batavia High sweatshirt, ashamed of the transparent lie she was about to tell. She knew and John Huey knew and Ronnie knew and Dominique knew where the shiner came from.

"A nigger on a bike hit me when I was carryin' groceries this morning."

She stared at the puke-green carpet, seeded with ubiquitous cookie crumbs.

"A nigger, huh? Bastard. I oughta kill him." Ronnie's dudgeon had a forced, perfunctory quality. He scowled for a while, for effect. Gradually he worked up his ire.

"A nigger, huh?," he repeated. "Who?" He bore down on John Huey, demanding, "Who? Who? Who? Who?"

John Huey stared at Ronnie's hands, bathed in grease and ineffably muscular—how does a man develop powerful fingers?

"I don't know," the neighbor in 132 squealed, afraid that Stanley Kowalski was about to strangle him. "I just came over to say hi and introduce myself to your wife." That came out wrong.

"Oh," Ronnie cried in the universal bully mock-falsetto, "you just came over to introduce yourself to my wife. How nice. My name, in case you care, is Ronnie." He shook John Huey's hand. It was sore when he let go. "And this is my lovely wife Wanda. Our lovely daughter Dominique is outside right now, giving head to nine-year-old niggers. Now get your ass outta my house." He pointed to the door.

John Huey offered a weak "if you need anything, Wanda, you know where I am," and slunk out.

Dominique was standing outside the screen door, hearing all.

"Hi, little princess, how are you?" he smiled, stopping for an esteem-building chat, but she'd listened to his craven performance and just shrugged her shoulders, unwilling to pardon pusillanimity.

When John Huey got home he heard a woman's wail, tremulous and piercing. He shut the windows and buried his head in his pillow, vainly attempting to achieve absolution through ignorance.

It was a hot Indian summer afternoon at the West End Bar and Grill. John Huey was staring into his beer, trying to control the surging anger he felt for the dumbass patrons sitting next to him laughing uproariously at the allegedly ribald bleeps and blunders TV special. At fifteen-minute intervals the program was interrupted by beer commercials depicting heartland Americans as seen through the skewed eyes of cocaine-snorting Manhattan advertising executives. The handsome models on the TV screen sat on tractors, rotated tires, wooed tomboys, wore hardhats, dribbled basketballs between their legs, and walked proudly out of factory doors. John Huey wondered if the men at the bar recognized themselves.

He felt a stinging slap on his back, which he hated, though not as much as when some sack of shit came up from behind, grabbed him in a chokehold with a forearm blindfold, and said, "Guess who?" Now he felt a palm crack his back, and in the same swamp-inflected voice of his boyhood, the Great Hunt—jockocrat ruler of the Class of '78—said, "Hey, Huuuuu-eeeee, how you doin' man?"

The advance man of his welcoming party.

He turned around to a bleary-eyed Hunt, who studied John Huey dumbly, as if he were an English test, then wrought a weak facsimile of his famous rotten-toothed smile. He was fat; well, not fat but about twenty-five pounds over his playing weight. John Huey could see that Hunt's hair was falling out and knew that would bother him, 'cause it really does bother all guys.

Hunt sat down, and without any prompting slurred out his life story. Usually this kind of shit bored John Huey senseless, but seeing the end result of the prototypical Batavia metamorphosis—teen idol turned adult idle, a wretched drunk on the downbound train—so emphatically confirmed his world view that he bought them both Gennys and listened with rapt, lurid attention.

Hunt's rambling monologue lasted maybe an hour, interrupted by two urgent trips to the men's room:

"Goddam, man, I ain't seen you in a fuckin' coon's age. . . . How the fuck you been? . . . Shee-it, the times man, man they change. You know what the fuck I'm doin' now? . . . Goddam, I'm a fuckin' janitor at Batavia Fucking High. . . . Shit, man, sweepin' the goddam floors. . . . And you know what, man? (jabs him with a finger) You wanna know fuckin' what? . . . All this pussy, juicy tight dago pussy, walkin' them halls while I sweep the fuckers. . . . They won't even talk to me! . . . Fuckin' lowlife, how's they see me. Fuckin' janitor, not good enough, not good enough to talk to. . . . Stuck-up little cunts. . . . Yeah, man, I'm married. Fuck-ing married. Wife, two kids. . . . Shee-it. . . . Naw, you don't know her. Tammy Henderson, she's two years behind us, from Pembroke. Shit, I didn't even love her, just fucked her once, maybe twice, she gets knocked up, goddam. . . . Ah, I tell ya Huuuu, things man, things don't work out the way they're supposed to, ya know? . . . Sweepin' the goddam floors, shit, even cleanin' out the goddam toilets with shit'n'stuff in 'em. . . . Marry a horny twat and two months later she turns into a fat bitch . . . Christ, man, I fucked up my life . . . (pause) . . . you know, man, you would probably classify me as a alcoholic. [*No, Hunt!*] Yeah, yeah, man, I get off work, four-thirty, walk over here. I got my goddam license suspended for fucking DWI, they're really crackin' down on that shit. . . . Man, walk over here and drink myself into fuckin' oblivion. Big Bad Hunt. Alcoholic janitor."

Hunt drained his brew, and they knocked back a couple tequilas. John Huey slapped down a two-bill tip and stood to leave. A tear—the thick, gelatinous kind you see rolling down diseased, varicose old cheeks—slipped from Hunt's rheumy left eye. John Huey started to say good-bye, but by now Hunt was long, long gone, stuffing that Olympia ball carrier on fourth and goal at the one again, and again, and again, as ever it shall be.

EXCERPT FROM JOHN HUEY'S JOURNAL

Convene the doctors, the lawyers, the smug plutocracy, the sociologists, the actresses, *The New York Times*, Westchester mistresses, editorial writers, all those who take privilege and position for granted. A crisis impends—a looming demographic/taxonomic threat that menaces the very foundations of your social aerie.

Listen up! The poor, the downtrodden, the proles, the white-trash inmates of trailer parks, are stealing your names. *Your motherfucking names!* The barbarian

Demos is loose, stirring up rebellion in Appellation City. And the culprit—aha, justice be served—is what you had thought to be a useful opiate: TV.

Tour the maternity wards of the lower middle class. Count the Brunos, the Butches, the Ediths, even the Bobs and Bills and Joes and Freds and Larrys and Marys and Marthas and Helens and Lindas. You can do it on two hands.

Now wander those smudged halls and discover the Jacquelines and Fallons and Nicoles and Ashleys and Melissas. There's enough to fill a Hormel plant! (I know, because the trash-waif daughter of my slut neighbor is not, as the natural order enjoins, a Cherlynne or Candy or Peggy or, if to the manor born, a Mary Anne, but rather . . . Dominique! Named, I think, after the ebony bitch who used to be on *Dynasty*.)

So. The subversive implications of this widespread—this *pandemic*—name-usurping by the teeming masses deserve careful study. I never like to hazard predictions, at least not in print, but I will share with you an apocalyptic vision of mine. It is twelve years hence, on a grassy lot adjoining the Batavia junior high school. A circle of denimed teenaged girls is seen inhaling cigarettes. Most will end their education the day they turn sixteen, the lucky ones falling into $4.50-an-hour textile jobs, the unlucky ones begetting illegitimate children, the imbeciles opting for prostitution or worse. A cop routs them, more for cheap scabrous thrills than anything else, and writes their names in his ringed memo pad. Their surnames are a polyglot lot, but their Christian (?) names are . . . identical to your daughters'! *Exactly the same.* And you can't change them, or erase them, or alter the rules in the middle of the game. You're stuck in nomenclature hell for the rest of your days. You, and Alexis, and Meredith, and Courtney.

Wanda meeting John Huey at the biker-infested Blondy's (sic) Bar was pure fortuity—or so she assured him.

"I can't believe you're here," she said, tapping his shoulder. "I come here once in a while, but I never seen you."

He assumed she was lying; at least he hoped so.

"Here, have a seat," he urged.

"Okay. Thanks."

The bearish, bearded bartender, whose forearm tattoo— "Fuck U2"—belied a gracious, concerned manner, set up two draft beers. It dawned on John Huey that his evening, with its scheduled lugubrious intoxicated reflection, was shifting focus. He wondered how onerous the conversational burden might be.

"So," Wanda began, inauspiciously, "what's up?"

He hated that question. Its open-endedness admitted no response. Hell, lots of things were up.

"Not too awfully much." He longed for her to undertake an extended disquisition upon some aspect, any aspect, of her wretched and abject life. He wanted to drink.

"How 'bout you?"

"Oh, not a lot. Dominique came home today with a note from her teacher sayin' that she was too wild, she needed to settle down and stop makin' so much noise and always talkin' and stuff." She sipped her beer and smiled. "I don't know where she gets that from."

John Huey forced an appreciative laugh. Boring people always want to be told that they're crazy and wild and uninhibited.

"How's Ronnie?"

"Ronnie," she blubbered, spitting a half-raspberry. "Ronnie can go fuck himself, excuse my French."

The profanity turned him on. He wanted to hear more.

"Why do you say that?"

She released a lengthy, nigh interminable sigh. She brushed a dangling burnt-yellow bundle of hair out of her eyes. She drank deeply, dutifully, of the beer, draining the glass. She nodded to the tattooed barkeep for a refill. She pulled her stool closer to John Huey's, so that the brass bases touched. She spoke.

"Ronnie is an asshole. He beats me. I didn't get that black eye the other day from a nigger, I got it from Ronnie. Sometimes, when he's not drinkin', when things at work are goin' OK, when softball season is goin' on, he's fine. He treats me good, calls me darling, takes me out to dinner at Chicken Kitchen on Friday night. Everything's real cool then, plus he plays with Dominique and treats her real good. And he sleeps with me too.

"But other times, most of the time now, it seems, he's a jerk. He comes home when he feels like it, I smell all kinds of liquor on his breath, and he bosses me around and no matter what I say or do he hits me. Really hard, too, he's got a real punch, and sometimes he'll leave for the night and go sleep with one of his whores, one of those sluts at Riley's, or sometimes he'll come home and make me sleep with him. And when he sleeps with me sometimes he rapes me. That might sound funny, a husband raping his wife, but he does it, and once I screamed 'cause I thought he was gonna hurt me and I woke up 'Nique and she came running into the bedroom and screaming, crying . . . she didn't know what was goin' on. And Ronnie gets offa me and grabs her, real hard, by the arm and lifts her up and he's screamin' at her — 'Shut the fuck up! Shut the fuck up!' — and he carries her by the arm like she's a rag doll back into her room, then he comes back in and. . . . Well, he abused me, sexually, I thought for a second he was gonna kill me."

"Why don't you just pack up Dominique and leave the asshole?" John Huey wanted to ask, but he didn't. He felt sure that her answer would be lifted from the lexicon of TV, from one of those dreadfully earnest socially conscious Hollywood melodramas, where rapists and murderers and wife-beaters have "problems" that are cured when the sinner "admits the problem to himself."

He wondered if Wanda, or any in her milieu, was capable of articulating feelings or beliefs in her own language; or whether pop culture, like a thoroughgoing imperialist, had substituted its vocabulary for the natural, simpler language of the people. If Wanda said that Ronnie "needs help," would she be expressing an independent opinion born of reflection and experience, or would she be parroting a combination of words, a formula, that her authoritative, ever-loquacious guest, Television, had recommended?

While John Huey pondered these Big Questions, Wanda sang soft accompaniment to the song blasting from the jukebox. She sang intently, maybe even passionately, enunciating the stanzas as well as the chorus.

John Huey had heard the song before: "Who Will You Run To?" by a bombastic female-fronted band named Heart. He'd never bothered to decipher the lyrics, writing off Heart and mainstream, popular rock bands like it with the three Vs—vacant, vapid, vacuous. Greasy-haired boys washing Camaros in lumpensuburban front yards dug that shit; DC's New Class, even those abundantly ignorant of the musical landscape, opted for arty or arch, self-consciously ironic bands, *e.g.*, Talking Heads. No convivial gathering of Young Republicans or Young Democrats was complete without a sloshed Georgetown girl yelling "put on some Heads," and the host(ess) readily obliging, the inaugural chords of "Life During Wartime" activating a sweaty, affluent mass of dancers.

But in Batavia, Heart dominated the jukebox. John Huey strained to hear Wanda's defiantly sung echolalia. Above a martial and inexorable beat, swollen to a crescendo at each refrain, the throaty vocalist sang of abandonment, of betrayal, of the salvific properties of love:

You don't know what it's like to live on your own
You've always had me there beside you

You think it's easy to find someone out there
Who's gonna care as much as I do
What's gonna happen baby when you find out
There's no one left to cry to
You can tell the whole world how you're gonna make it
You can follow your heart
But what do you do when someone breaks it
Who will you run to when it all falls down
Who's gonna lift your world up off of the ground
Who's gonna take away the tears you cry
Who's gonna love you baby as good as I?

"I love that song," Wanda blurted as Heart's refrain faded. "I just love it."

"Why?" John Huey asked, reproaching himself immediately. She obviously liked it because it spoke to her life, resonantly, in ways that he could never understand. John Huey wished that he was an empathetic friend rather than a detached observer. Lording it over the likes of Wanda wasn't exactly the abnegation he'd sought.

"Oh, I don't know," she answered, "it just seems so . . . true."

"Hmmm," he grunted, ready to change the subject. No such luck.

"I feel that the Wilson sisters, Ann and Nancy, who are the singers in Heart, are singing words that apply to my life," said Wanda, picking up momentum. "It's like everybody in the world has the same experiences, everybody goes through the same things, and it's comforting, you know, that other people are in the same boat as you." She finished her beer and signaled for another.

"The best books are the ones that tell you something you already know," declared John Huey, hating the Orwell allusion and hoping Wanda wouldn't think him a pompous jerk. He wondered what Bertram Moost would think of this encounter.

"Yeah, that's true," said Wanda, wary that the discussion was taking a cerebral turn.

They drank warm refilled beers in awkward silence.

"John Huey?" Wanda's tone became assertive, fortified by alcohol.

"Yes'm?" (The Southern mimetic didn't amuse her, or make him seem cool.)

"What did you do in Washington? Did you have a good job, a government job? Did you have a girlfriend? What did you do?"

He weighed truth vs. embellishment vs. reticence. Should he be contrite, operatic, thoughtful, steely, or taciturn? His desire aroused by the third question in Wanda's artful series, he chose to play the classically laconic American male.

"Aw, I didn't do much. Some writing, mostly. I just discovered that it wasn't for me. And no, I didn't really have a steady girlfriend." His imp snickered at that last adjective.

"So you don't wanna tell me, huh? Okay, it's up to you. But if you ever wanna talk about it, about anything, just pop by. I like you. I'd like to talk to you."

Incredibly, he now feared boring her. The eve had peaked, he knew, and before bibulous confessions were spilled the couple had best vamoose. John Huey suggested leaving, and Wanda agreed.

They walked home, down empty nighttime streets, chatting about Wanda's job at Consolidated Packaging Inc. and Dominique's pretty face and, contrary to John Huey's terse intentions, he told amusing tales of drunken days of yore.

Finally, they arrived at her house.

"Well," pronounced John Huey, stupidly.

"Well," retorted Wanda.

"I guess I'll be seeing you tomorrow."

"Guess so."

John Huey so wanted to take her in his arms and kiss her. He harbored no slut-with-a-heart-of-gold fantasies; in the event, he doubted that Wanda fit that mold. Nor did he dream of whisking her away from poverty, filth, and ignorance, cleansing and edifying and educating the poor, plucky working class lass. Wanda wanted neither pity nor charity; her fatalistic acceptance of the tedium and defeats of everyday living removed her from the realm of patronizing savior conceits. (Or was John Huey imputing to her qualities that he *wished* her to have?)

He kissed her, heart amok, and bid her good-bye, running like crazy the fifty feet from her door to his. She'd taken his restraint—one closed-mouth, five-second kiss—for gallantry and valor; he knew it was a crippling case of nerves. Once home, he ran to his refrigerator, grabbed a beer, and sat down with his diary for a few moments before retiring to sweet Wanda dreams.

EXCERPT FROM JOHN HUEY'S JOURNAL

We walked down Elm Street, me hands in back pockets, posture-conscious, in need of a haircut; she a Slavic angel, laughing madly at embroidered tales of younger, punky days.

At her door we stopped, as here we went our separate ways. (She's married!) I opened my slit eyes wide and ran my right hand through my thinning (*No!*) hair, my sole nervous tic. I cleared my throat. She stepped off porch; I stayed on to emphasize male-female height difference.

"So," I said, mustering up my fake-bored rounder drawl, "you wanna get together again one of these days?"

"Yeah," she smiled.

(*You dope what's she gonna say you drooling sap she's standing right next to you eye to eye of course courtesy requires her to say yes.*)

I tried to give her a cute wide-eyed look, but for all I know I looked like a drunk impersonating a Mongoloid idiot.

"You sure?"

She smiled the truest, most perfect smile I have ever seen. "Are you kidding? [*You timorous faggot*] Of course I do!"

We made a date at Blondy's next week. Now it was one in the morning. Maybe the wind was rustling through the trees or maybe birds were chirping love songs or maybe the Canadian Air Force was strafing the street. I don't remember.

"So, I'll see you later." (*Did you steal these lines from Oscar Wilde you tongue-tripping dork?*)

My head jerked toward hers in gawky passion. We kissed a crooked kiss, mouths nearly missing, then pulled away in amative laughter.

I turned and walked to my door. I'd floated fifteen feet or so when she called out.

"John Huey?"

I turned to look at the prettiest girl in the world.

"You got my phone number, right?"

I was at a sufficient distance to be a rounder again.

"Yeah, baby, I got your number."

She cocked her head and scrunched up her nose and waved 'bye to me.

I skipped home, dancing around my sleeping bag to "Candy's Room," and even though I had to take a piss I enjoyed that dance.

9

He was failing his tests, every damn one of them.

"I can't even fucking mortify myself right," lamented John Huey in alcoholic reprobation. "I come here to Batavia to die in peace, and I end up buried alive, pounding the top of the fucking casket."

He fell into his orange vinyl beanbag chair, purchased for $3 at a yard sale in Cardboard City, and mopingly evaluated his Batavia hegira.

On the plus side were his bare apartment in a bleak housing project; his diminishing savings account; Hunt and Ronnie and the army of the undead; the utter indifference the town had shown to his existence; and the onset of the bitter, squalling winter months.

On the debit side, far outweighing the wanton dreariness of John Huey's Batavia, was Wanda.

Wanda, Wanda, Wanda . . . the abused semiliterate white-trash slattern next door. His cinnamon girl, cynosure of his eye, sinful, sexy black-eyed Susan.

He thought of her day and night, her numinous image peremptorily dismissing the self-loathing that John Huey was trying so hard to bring to its final, horrible maturation. Against the odious chain of lies and half-truths and forsaken forebears that bound, fettered, and defined John Huey's twenty-eight years, Wanda offered the flimsiest, most mundane resistance: "I like you."

These three words, her profession of faith, he clung to as a block of wood in a tumultuous ocean. He no longer wished to drown; yet he knew that his prospects on shore were hopeless and dismal.

Now and then John Huey thought of DC, of Bertram, of Solley, of the cranky Idaho newsman who was his number-one fan. He realized that a return was impossible, but he couldn't help occasionally daydreaming about a new column, new prominence, perhaps even a new ideology. And, of course, a new mate: Wanda in hip-huggers and golden earrings and beribboned, desnarled hair, toasting John Huey's Man of the Year citation at the American Foundation. Chatting with Bertram about Burke, with Krull about a raise, with tomorrow's matrons about Georgetown real estate. . . .

"And with Fred about his perfidious asshole grandson?" The imp knocked John Huey back to terra Batavia and left him huddling in his beanbag chair with shame and guilt and a renewed sense of betrayal. Was Wanda, too, a ductile plaything, to be shaped and molded into a sham, counterfeit impostor, a malleable means to John Huey's ambitious, arid ends?

He curled into the fetal position and begged God (if You are up there) and Fred (wherever you are) and Wanda (please don't find me out) for forgiveness.

His coffin had plenty of air, he now understood. He resolved to teach himself to stop pounding against it.

———

They sat in Wanda's darkened living room, which was suffused with the dim yellow light thrown by the banker's lamp atop an old family bureau. The house was haphazardly decorated, sturdy native desks and dressers (heirlooms, no doubt) coexisting with cheap bric a brac and poorly upholstered vinyl chairs. John Huey tried to convince himself that Wanda's simple homespun class had been violated by Ronnie's overlaid vulgarity—that the oak buffet was hers, the torn Charlie's Angels poster (original trio) and coffee-stained *TV Guide* were his—but he knew that the furniture and adornments represented a harmonious blend of WandaRonnie, not a rebarbative admixture.

The swelling over her left eyelid had abated, or so it seemed, and in the weak light she looked almost pretty. Wanda was thin but not, as John Huey thought at their first meeting, frail. Hers was a wiry toughness—an angular tension that suggested resilience and maybe even pluck.

She had moxie.

Her blonde hair was unwashed: he imagined running a comb through it and encountering stubborn knots and tangles at every passage. But Wanda wasn't dirty so much as weary. In thirty years she'd been crunched and boxed and hammered and raped and spit out by all manner of personal and impersonal forces. And she wasn't gonna wash her hair just because another sunrise presented itself.

"I want you to see what Ronnie used to look like, so you won't think he's a total monster." She opened an immaculately preserved yearbook—emblazoned *Oakfield Hornets '76*—and laid it across her lap.

John Huey expected a sullen manchild glaring amidst an assemblage of high-school shop students. He was wrong.

His second guess was a cocky jock wearing the fluffy equine coif of the day. Bingo.

"Ronnie Fay. Football 9, 10, 11, 12. Baseball 9, 10, 11. Basketball 9, 10, 11, 12. O-A-Boys Club 11, 12. Memories: cruzin' at Jasper's, BoHay, Notre Dame game, Skynyrd, turkey in the bushes, Janine."

John Huey wondered whatever happened to Janine but didn't want to abrade any open wounds. Wanda was staring at the two-by-three yearbook photo of Ronnie in a contrast-stitching leisure suit.

"What happened to senior baseball?" An obvious question.

Wanda, distractedly, replied, "Oh, he got in some trouble. Smokin' a joint in the boys room or sumpin'. Nothing too bad. He was a party guy back then."

Before John Huey could formulate a second line of inquiry,

she disappeared, reemerging a minute later with a dog-eared scrapbook embossed with *The Times of Our Lives*.

She skimmed it rapidly, searching for her favorite photo: Ronnie in his Little League uniform, crouching in wait for an imagined grounder.

"Wasn't he a cute kid?" she asked, and her grin dissolved into a hiccupping laugh which uncorked a freshet of tears. She placed her head in her hands and sobbed buckets.

"It's OK," John Huey reassured her, though he didn't know what was OK or why it was OK or if that which was OK could ever be set right.

He wanted to comfort her, to console her, to condole with her, but his arm balked at encircling her shoulders. He sat there, awkwardly staring while Wanda wept, and he felt deep shame when an erection threatened. He tried to shove any lustful—or romantic—feelings out of his heart. He failed.

Ashamed by the stirrings below, he lifted the scrapbook from Wanda's lap and inspected the contents. Ronnie at three, overwhelmed by a conical fireman's hat. Ronnie at six, a scared little man being pushed out the door by mom for his first day of school. Ronnie at ten, expertly dropping clothespins into a milk bottle. Ronnie at fifteen, limber and athletic, waving a tinpot trophy as his radiant mom looks on. Ronnie at twenty-three, baby in his arms, expressionless. Or maybe it just looked that way.

John Huey was taken with the Little League picture. Ronnie was almost cherubic, his round boy's face an American archetype. There was life behind those eyes, thought John Huey, a curious and vivacious late-'60s Huck Finn who hit homeruns and giggled at *Playboy* and probably even liked a teacher or two on the sly.

When John Huey left, Wanda was still crying. He walked down Dewey Avenue in the crow-black midnight, clearing that damned frog in his throat with mighty exertions, and then he walked back, wondering how a freckled boy in a Little League uniform could grow up to be a brute of nigh-inhuman dimension.

He walked for days and nights on end, unforgetting his past. In Centennial Park, under the ancient elms with their reddening autumnal leaves, he learned the constellations. He'd sit at the park's crest and watch Venus magically appear in the twilight sky. He had seen it through a telescope once, a fuzzy dot stained by a blue filter. He had not liked how our celestial neighbor had looked in reflected glass; one night in the park, he spent hours refereeing a debate in his mind. Resolved: that scientists are the despoilers of the heavens.

A cloudy night in October, the sky closed to watchers, John Huey stayed home. He sprawled out in his beanbag chair, belly down, shifting his weight and favoring his sore knee and pulling his dampened socks and altogether acting a fastidious prissy.

Nighttime. A harsh, shrill wind shrieked outside his door, blowing great gusts of early snow through Cardboard City, easily as a youngster dispersing a clump of dust with a single puff. Late October had arrived, and she was demanding obeisance.

John Huey temporized for a few minutes more, spreading a bland imitation cheese paste over stale crackers and washing the lump down his throat with an ice-cold Genny. He repositioned himself on his solitary furnishing, drew a breath, and opened the file labeled Huey Long/ Grandpa.

Tomorrow was Fred's birthday—the eighty-second anniversary of his appearance on the world stage—yet it suggested no celebration. John Huey was the final Ketchum, after all, the end of an unlamented, unremarkable, unprepossessing bloodline, so a party or family gathering was out of the question. And Fred had hated the church and its agents with sheer, coruscating intensity, eternally convinced that the priests were "in it for the money." Memorial services, therefore, would be high blasphemy.

No commemoration was planned in the flat, hard town in which Fred had been born, lived all his life, and died. The men and women with whom he worked and spoke and spent his days all remembered Fred from time to time: his earthen disposition, his resolute and uncompromising sense of right and wrong, his astonishing gentleness and generosity toward friends and family. Their warm memories and enriched lives consecrated the unholy Fred in a thousand different ways and means, thought John Huey: even the least of his surviving friends had never traded on Fred's name or recast the plain facts of Fred's corporeal existence.

He opened the file, a thin, disorganized collection of Huey Long clippings and memorabilia and rare examples of Fred's handwriting. (Fred wrote virtually nothing: he even disliked signing his name on the back of his Social Security check, God knows why.)

John Huey flipped through the file, stopping, remembering, conjecturing whenever an item piqued his interest. For instance:

—The sheet music to Long's composition "Every Man a King."

> Why weep or slumber, America?
>   Land of brave and true
> With castles, clothing, and food for all
>   All belongs to you
>
> Ev'ry man a king, ev'ry man a king
>   For you can be a millionaire
> But there's something belonging to others
> There's enough for all people to share
> When it's sunny June and December, too
> Or in the wintertime or spring
> There'll be peace without end
> Ev'ry neighbor a friend
>   With ev'ry man a king

A pleasing song, less exquisite and dainty than Cole Porter, say, but also realer—no mannered, detached, parlor cleverness for Huey.

John Huey couldn't imagine Fred singing this ditty, no matter how well lubricated. Singing was for sissies. But listening wasn't, and he saw a beaming, soul-stirred Fred, beating time on his knee, Share Our Wealth button stuck to his thick, wide lapel, baby (Dad!) bouncing on his lap, Irish saint wife exercising her sweet mellifluous Cork voice to please her young husband. A handsome tableau.

—Xeroxed pages of Long's *My First Days in the White House*, a remarkable excursion into braggadocio and radical populism. (Huey promised to make pacifist ex-General Smedley D. Butler his Secretary of War, quite a trick for a "home-grown fascist," Long's role in American mythology.)

Had Fred read the book straight through? John Huey imagined the faint light of a kerosene lamp illuminating the pages, Fred diligently studying the antiplutocratic polemics, guiltily skipping the confusing tax chapters.

—A small white celluloid button ("Share Our Wealth/ Every Man a King") pinned to a letter. Written on crisp, decomposing United States Senate stationery, the note read:

DEAR MR. KETCHUM:
Thank you so much for starting a Share Our Wealth club in Gennessee [sic] County. Every Man A King! I say and I have enclosed my autobiography and information about Share Our Wealth and my homestead plan. All the facts and figures you'll need! There's lots of suckers in Washington, and I bet there ain't nearly so many up in Gennessee County. Every Man a King, in Louisiana and New York.
  SINCERELY YOURS,
  Huey P. Long
  Senator

John Huey wondered if Long's barely legible scrawl was authentic, or the mechanical work of an autopen. He tried to imagine Fred's excitement at seeing the Senate envelope in his mailbox; upon reading the homey, hail-fellow-well-met text; upon coming to the handwritten name of Huey Pierce Long, the Kingfish, whose rabble-rousing Fred wished to transplant from the bayous of Louisiana to the smoldering colony of upper York State.

Fred would have read it before telling Grandma, surely, to save embarrassment if the letter was cursory or obviously machine-generated. And, oh! the glint in Grandma's eye when she saw that the basso voice on the radio, the remote, famous Huey P. Long, had written her husband, the loyal lieutenant, the janitor with the assured, natural bearing of the rough-hewn American.

—Finally, there was the birthday card.

It arrived a week before the first birthday John Huey spent in Washington. The envelope bore the addressee's name in the careful block printing of the infrequent penman. The card hadn't the usual florid or groovy illustration, just a plain *Happy Birthday* in bold red letters.

Inside, in labored printing, a note read:

Dear John Huey:

Happy Birthday to you. I hope you have a fine day. Do you like Washington? Do you like it more than home? Do what you think is right but I hope you will come home. I miss you.

Grandpa

Rereading it for the first time in years, John Huey wept. Tears flooded his eyes and streamed down his face as he recalled the countless phone conversations with Fred, all ending with the old man imploring, "Come home, John Huey, come home. Washington isn't for you, that's not your place, you belong right back here in Batavia."

He'd humor the old man: "Yeah, Grandpa, yeah, you're right, I'll probably be coming home one of these days."

Well, he had returned, just as Fred had wished, years late and for all the wrong reasons. Fred died disappointed, he felt certain, alone and abandoned by the little tad who bore his imprint.

And the little deserter, not content with killing the old man with heartbreak, proceeded to dance and piss and shit and puke all over the grave, dressing and primping and cosmeticizing the skeleton with all the gay insouciance of a necro-hairdresser. Did Fred rest in peace, John Huey wondered, or did his anguished soul pace the corridors of populist heaven, bewailing to one and all the base character of his asshole grandson?

"I'm home, Grandpa," whispered John Huey, the bitter, salty taste of his tears stinging his tongue. "I'm home."

―――

It made for a picture of startling incongruity: Ronnie sitting on the hood of his coupe, *reading a book*.

The vespertine setting of the October sun—mellow, ripe, comfortable in its old age—was a bravura performance. The bare deciduous trees had lapped up the sunlight as a scurvy, starving man consumes a banquet feast; unchained dogs scampered wildly across yards, spastic with delight at fall's reprieve. And Ronnie's swollen but sculpted body curled languidly about the Dodge's hood as he drank the pages with all the studious fervor of a young Emily Dickinson.

John Huey, who'd carefully avoided the brute since their black-eye encounter, felt all wariness and caution melt under the ardor of his curiosity. Watching Ronnie's comings and goings—the swaggering bluster, the drunken threats, the vulgar oaths, the pathetic and frightening weaving midnight walks—had convinced John Huey that Wanda's wayward husband was some base, subhuman parody of the T-shirted working-class male. Was his assessment wrong? Did the exaggerated, brawling, *mean* macho veneer hide a gentle and sensitive soul, straining, perhaps, to be at last understood?

John Huey ambled over to his neighbor's car. The hood on the hood, engrossed in his book, didn't look up.

"Hey, Ron, how's it goin'?" offered John Huey with forced casualness.

Ronnie looked up, inserting his right forefinger as a bookmark.

"OK. Yourself?"

"Oh, not bad, not bad at all. This weather's somethin', huh?"

"Yeah."

John Huey admired the unself-conscious brevity of Ronnie's answers. Anyone else would fear being mistaken for retarded.

"Whatcha readin'?" John Huey's mind was alive with a

thousand possible responses. Say Tennyson, Ron, say Tennyson!

"Book about the Lottery," answered Ronnie, glad to be asked. "It tells you how to win. Or at least it gives you advice and tells you the strategies that other people have used to win in different states."

Ah, applied mathematics, noted the imp. Though John Huey knew nothing about lotteries, he wondered what energies Ronnie channeled into his gamesmanship. He pressed on.

"Do you play the Lottery? What is it, every week, every month . . . ?"

Ronnie sat upright, interested in sharing his passion, even with a questioner he'd called a "fuckin' wimp" in an argument with his wife.

"I play it every day. Usually I play the Big Six; sometimes I play Baseball or Lotto. I spend about eighty, ninety bucks a week, so I bought this book to see if my luck might change."

The amount staggered John Huey. Ronnie couldn't bring home more than $180, $190 weekly. Ronnie anticipated the unoffered question.

"That's a lotta money. But I hit some OK ones before—I made five hundred once, won two-fifty twice, a hundred twice, and a mess of fifties. So I don't lose too much. And I figure I could hit the big one—it changes what the amount is, sometimes it's only one or two million, once I think it got as high as thirty-five or forty million. But y'know, somebody's gotta win it, and I figure, heh, my chances are as good as the next guy. And if I use this book and learn some of the strategies, I figure I add to my chances and make the other guy's get smaller. So that's why I'm readin' this book."

John Huey laid a hand on this gospel of numerology, tilting the cover toward him to get a better look. *You can WIN the LOTTERY*, it advised immodestly; the author, Dr. Francine Bellagria, was a svelte, attractive woman, sandwiched by two Mercedes Benzes in a somewhat blurry photo at cover's bottom. The book appeared to be self-published. John Huey wondered whence Ms. Bellagria received her doctorate, and in what discipline.

"So," said John Huey, a note of condescension creeping into his voice, "does Dr. Francine have any good tips?"

Ronnie spit at the asphalt. "Yeah, she might." He betrayed a sudden coldness, which John Huey rushed to counteract.

"Well, I guess you're right, anybody could win that money." Ronnie had reopened the book and was paying his enlightened neighbor no mind.

"Tell me, Ron," said John Huey, taking a failsafe tack, "what would you do if you won thirty-five million dollars?"

Ronnie's attention remained fixed on the page. There was a long, uncomfortable silence before he spoke.

"I'd get the fuck outta here, that's for sure. I'd get the fuck outta Batavia and away from my job and Wanda and this fuckin' slum and every asshole in it, including you."

He sprang from the car, rubber soles hitting pavement as the book slammed shut. The suddenness, and his blunt grace, caused John Huey to recoil.

"Don't worry, shitass. I ain't gonna hit you. You ain't

worth it." He tapped the book with his knuckles. "I got more important things to do."

With that Ronnie threw his bible into the car, squeezed his frame into its cramped confines, gunned the engine, and peeled out of Cardboard City, hitting the kiddie-bumps at fifty miles per hour, jangling the car's insides and soaring a good eighteen inches before the abrupt flight ended and the fenders came crashing down to earth.

John Huey stood at the bar of Riley's Friendly Tavern, venerable watering hole for five generations of Batavians, listening, hearing:

"My wife, hah! Fuck the bitch!"

"Man, the Bills better not sign Jefferson as backup. Nigger quarterback, can't even remember the plays, probably."

"Things slower than hell at the plant, slow as hell. They're talkin' about a big order from Germany comin' in, but I don't see it. I don't see it at all."

"Two more brewskis, Shep."

"Man, am I fucked up."

"I ain't gonna put up with any more of his shit. I just ain't."

"I wish I could. Really I wish I could. But I can't. I got work, y'know. There's lots of things I'd like to do, but I just can't. I'm sorry."

"Seven-seven."

"Hey, Billy, how's it goin'?"

"President Asshole can suck my wang."

"I can't believe about Pete. When I heard, I just, I just, you know, sat there. Sat there for like half an hour just thinkin', thinkin' about all the times we used to go out, playin' street hockey, thinkin' about the time we got kicked out of the library. We were some crazy bastards. . . . I still can't believe it. Just to think that one minute he was here, he was here, now who knows where he is. I just can't handle that death stuff."

"Aww, I gotta go to work tomorrow."

"Let's do some shooters, buddy."

"Yup. DWI."

"Iron Fuckin' Maiden."

"You're fulla shit, man. Play Randy Travis. I'll even give ya the goddam quarter."

"Hey, do you remember that Yankees game where they picked Winfield off first two times in a row? Sheeesh."

"I'd ask her out, but I don't know if she likes me."

"No. Get outta here. . . ."

"Yeah, wasn't that weird?"

"Hey, man, you're usin' a busted cue."

"Whatta ya have?"

"Sometimes Kim gets on my nerves, I get really pissed at her, we have these fights, once she threw this hardened-up frozen fish, yeah, really, she threw a fish at me, and it hit the wall and split in two. Jeee-zuz Christ. But still, Chuck, a man needs a woman. She's my partner, I know that sounds corny, but she is. I can't talk to her about things because men, you know, men, we're trained from childhood not to show our feelings. That's hard, you know, so I keep all this stuff inside me, but still, for the stuff I can actually talk to her about, it's a good feeling. I don't know. When are you gonna get married?"

"I gotta take a wicked piss."

"Remember the time. . . ."

When John Huey was young his dad told him a story about Riley's, a tale he'd never forgotten. It seems that in the late '30s, Batavia had one hell of a town baseball team. "Townball" was a semipro deal, with the top nine from one village playing neighboring jockocracies every Saturday afternoon from May till Labor Day. Games were the social highlight of the summer: virtually the whole town would turn out, and as the years passed every matchup became laden with its own peculiar history. The mythopoeic aspect of sport combined with the chauvinism of the town to spawn a welter of lore and legend and lies and exaggeration, all recycled and refurbished with the passing of each summer Saturday.

The star of the prewar Batavia teams was O. D. Lear, a squat, balding black man whose thirty-six-inch bat deposited a cannonade of white pellets into the thickets four hundred feet away in left-center. Except for a squealing, staccato laugh, Lear was an unremarkable fellow, neither a dissolute bum nor a Noble Negro. He was just a guy.

After Batavia games, the team and its retinue repaired to Riley's to drink the night away. Toasts were made, oaths were sworn, trysts were scheduled, aging youth boozily contemplated the onset of mediocrity. As it is today.

O. D. Lear, though he swam in the invisible Negro pool of West Batavia, always partook of the postgame festivity—and submitted to its rites. You see, coach Pepper Stark invariably ordered a round of whiskeys for the boys, win or lose. Players and coach formed a semicircle, raised their shot glasses, and roared, "Onward, upward, inward, Batavia," downing the booze to the applause of bystanders. After the ceremony, old man Riley collected the glasses. He'd bring them to the kitchen for washing—all but one, that is. For every summer Saturday—and my father attested to this, and I believe him—Riley, in full view of his tavern's patrons, would toss O. D. Lear's shot glass into an unused fireplace, shattering it to pieces. "I don't have nuthin' against a nigger drinkin' in my place," explained Riley, "but I sure as hell ain't gonna let the glass that his lips touched get used by white customers."

Since he first heard this story, John Huey had wondered about the details. Did O. D. Lear protest? Did any of his teammates? Why did O. D. keep coming back? Did Riley feel a twinge of compunction at this recurring public scourging? Did the two men meet years later, bent, crippled, and wise, and laugh about it? Or did O. D. forever harbor secret revenge fantasies? Why, Lord, why?

John Huey never knew.

10

"Ronnie split," Wanda said matter-of-factly, twirling the telephone cord around her index finger. "He said the world was caving in on him, and then he packed up his clothes in his suitcase and left."

"Where'd he go?" John Huey hoped it was the other end of the planet.

"His sister's house on Kibbe Avenue"—a site short of Timbuctoo.

"Jeez, if he's makin' such a big deal about suffocating and Time for Me to Fly and all that bullshit, how come his big move spans approximately nine hundred yards?"

"I dunno. That's just Ronnie. He ain't ever been outta this

area, except when him and his buddies go to Canada to see the nude strippers."

"Still, it seems to me that if he's so beleaguered he'd want to at least leave town."

"Yeah, seems so."

Pause.

"How you doin'?"

"Fine. He didn't hit me or anything. I'm kinda relieved, to tell you the truth."

"Is there anything I can do?"

"Yeah."

"What?"

"Come over here."

She met him at the door with a hug, whether for solace or seduction he did not know. They sat on the couch.

"So," said John Huey, nervous, "where's Dominique? How's she taking it?"

"Oh, 'Nique's at school, of course. She's happy, I s'pose. She don't like to see her momma get beat to a pulp."

John Huey's mind frantically raced for conversation topics. He wanted nothing more in the world than to make love to Wanda; nothing terrified him so much.

"So, I guess you're happy that it's finally over. Or do you think it's over?"

"Yeah," Wanda sighed. "It's over. He's packed up his clothes before, but he never took his goddam sports trophies till yesterday. He took 'em. So he ain't comin' back."

"I wish I'd gotten to know Ronnie better," John Huey lied, as phantasmal close-ups of his abrupt and only sexual experience raced through his head. His body had gone limp with fright. He was too numb even to shake, rattle, and quaver, his usual boy-meets-girl dance.

"No," she protested, "Ronnie was an asshole. He coulda learned a lot more from you than you coulda from him."

Wanda started giggling; she put her hand to her mouth, as if to stanch the flow, but the dike burst and she was overcome with great waves and torrents of laughter. She doubled over and smothered her face in the couch seat. After a minute or so of muffled outbursts, she resumed normal breathing, punctuated by fugitive giggles. She was now sprawled across the length of the couch, her feet overhanging one arm rest (her long, jagged toenails on display), her head snuggled against John Huey's lap. He felt an erection building, and he knew that all the dead rotting nun carcasses and all the counting backwards from 100 by fives couldn't stop this one.

"Uh, what was so funny?" he asked, vainly attempting to shift his thickening dick from underneath the crown of her head.

"Oh, I was just thinkin'."

"About what?"

"About how when Ronnie left he said I'd be sorry for bein' such a bitch that drove him to hit me cause 'There aren't two guys in this whole fucking town that are fit to carry my jock,' he said. Hah. I told him there are men in town he's never heard of and that he wasn't fit to live in the same universe with. 'Not in Cardboard City,' he said. 'Wanna bet?' I said. And now I'm just comparin' you and him, and believe me, there ain't no contest."

Her arms reached for his neck. She gently guided his head down to meet hers. She greeted him with a ravenous open-mouthed kiss, her tongue excavating the roof of his mouth so thoroughly that for a second he feared he'd swallow his own tongue and hers too.

"Come with me," she whispered in his ear, sucking the lobe, and she led him to the unmade bed. She ripped off her shirt and pants, and before the standing John Huey could unbutton his flannel shirt she'd slid his pants down and was planting those same French kisses upon his penis.

He tried a graceful descent into bed, fearful that her earnest fellatio was going to cut his second carnal experience as short as the first, but she blocked his path, unwilling to surrender her unaccustomed position of controller/director/navigator of the sexual act.

By now his eyes were shut, his balled fists clamped her temples, and he murmured, "OhOhOhOhOhOh," his resistance-borne-of-teenage-abjection melting with each moist kiss, until he surrendered unto the lonely temptress, thy neighbor's wife.

As his senses cleared, the dread feel of sexual ineptness overcame him. Squalid failure, again! Without so much as an eight-ounce beer to blame.

He looked down and saw Wanda kissing his knees, improbably; the pottage of crumpled trousers and underpants that ringed his ankles resembled the flotsam of some sordid latrine encounter. Must his undisciplined hair-trigger cock screw up these decennial performances?

No excuse presented itself, so as John Huey fell to the bed,

Wanda wrapped around his legs, he readied an apology. "Wanda," he began, but she interrupted him with a "Shhhh," while shimmying up his torso, stopping when the lovers were face to face.

"Don't say anything, sweetie, please don't," she requested. "Don't thank me, or make a big deal about it, just lay back with me and relax. You seem the kind of guy that always . . . thinks about this stuff too much. I don't wanna turn it into a big intellectual thing. And you don't have to do anything to me. I don't care. I mean, I *do* care, but you don't have to do the big macho thing and drill me ten times this morning and ten times this afternoon. In the first place, nobody can do it that much, and in the second, I don't want you to get all nerved up, like you were playin' football on my body and all your buddies were watchin'. So just lie back and hold me, and we'll stay like this for as long as we want, and then we'll talk, and you can kiss me if you want."

With that she burrowed her head into the wedge between his jaw and collarbone, and they lay perfectly still, listening to the steps of the mailman, the shouts of truant boys, the peeling rubber of frustrated young James Deans who hadn't yet learned the futility of challenging the speedbumps. The lovers listened raptly to the exhalations and heartbeats of the God-made soul to which each had conjoined, so deliriously happy with their sudden union that neither felt the least urge to move. Their contented stillness lasted for hours, finally and smoothly seguing into a natural act of coitus that not even the most exacting sexual technician would consider abbreviated.

When Dominique came home from school she found her

bathrobed mother eating cereal at the kitchen table with a just-showered John Huey. She kissed her mother and hugged the neighbor, rubbing her button nose all over his hair, breathing in the fresh shampoo smell, intoxicated by the tranquil new presence that had supplanted her raging, bellicose father.

The fine smell of burning leaves betokened the arrival of Halloween.

A stout, older white woman, a dead ringer for Ma Joad, was walking the curvilinear streets of Cardboard City, picking up smashed pumpkin remains.

"Kids these days," she kept repeating to herself, the gourd fragments filling three, four, five large garbage bags. "Kids these days ain't go no respect for other people, no respect even for the little ones. Why do they have to go smashing the jack-o'-lanterns before Halloween night? Why do they have to be so destructive? Don't they care about other peoples' feelings?"

Dominique, little white-trash princess of Cardboard City, was dressed up as Miss New York State. Her scrawny eight-year-old body was draped in a crèpe robe. A dimestore tiara crowned her head. "Hey, John Huey," she shouted from her curbside seat as he walked into view, "look at me!"

She ran toward her mom's inamorato, stopping perhaps ten feet away and, after a graceful ruffles-and-flourishes bow, she pirouetted, clumsily, charmingly.

"I'm the beauty queen of Batavia," Dominique said triumphantly, to John Huey's vigorous assent. "Mommy says I'm the prettiest young thing she's ever seen." He agreed.

"Where's your mommy, honey, the second-prettiest thing I've ever seen?" Off she darted into her house, screaming "Mommy, mommy, John Huey's home."

Wanda met him at the door with a sloppy kiss; he had an immediate hard-on and wished to hell the kid was out trick-or-treating.

"Did you see Dominique's outfit?" she asked. "I made it, I kept it secret, I told her she'd have to just wear a sheet and go as Casper the Friendly Ghost. You shoulda seen her this morning when I showed it to her."

Wanda was damn near exultant, which got him even hotter, and he dumped the most fulsome load of praise you ever heard. "Jesus, baby, you know, you could've been some kind of designer in New York City if you put your mind to it. We're gonna have to celebrate your achievement in haute couture tonight."

She laughed, winked, flashed a lopsided and naughty grin, and went into the kitchen to pour a bag of mini-chocolate bars into a dish.

Then he realized: trick-or-treaters.

Doorbells all night.

A detumescent eve.

They took a few pictures of Miss Dominique, including one with John Huey on bended knee proposing marriage to the scraggly lass, before sending her on her way with a covey of witches and starlets and hula dancers and a four-year-old with a floppy banana sprouting from her head. White-trash flash.

It was dark by 6:30. The doorbell rang every five minutes, and Wanda would jump off the couch, open the door with candy-bar dish in hand, oooh and ahhh over the tatterdemalions and tramps shouting "Trick of treat!", close the door, and return to her TV-watching position, telling him "how cute" the kiddies were and how he ought to go to the door with her.

Halfway through the night John Huey realized that he'd never seen a trick-or-treater in Washington. It was, he thought, a ritual slain by the decay of family, the gentrification of once-homogeneous black neighborhoods, the . . . ah, fuck it, he mumbled. No sermons. Grinning, he apologized to himself. It's hard for a zombie to lose his pallor, y'know.

They could see the waxing crescent moon through the aperture that passed for Wanda's picture window. It quavered and trembled in the chill air. John Huey got up, blackened the lights, shut off the stupid goddam celebrity-gossip TV show, and lit the pumpkin they'd carved the weekend before. They reclined on the couch and he was a smooth, urbane seducer, worlds away from the bumbling premature ejaculator of his youth.

The doorbell rang several times over the next hour, but no one answered it. Wanda and John Huey made love by the orangish light of the pumpkin, and it may have been his imagination, but he thought he'd tired her out.

"Do you think I'm a slut?"

Wanda lay naked across John Huey's abdomen, her left hand caressing his right thigh.

"No." He answered impassively, as if she'd offered him a 7–Up.

Wanda reached for a warm Diet Coke on the nightstand. (All lower-middle-class girls keep tepid cans of pop handy till drinking fits strike, after which consumption the cans metamorphose into ashtrays.)

She sipped the Diet Coke while lying sideways, dribbling a brownish stream into the bed linen. She tried to recall the confessional she'd composed that afternoon at the laundromat.

"Y'know," Wanda began, nestling her head into John Huey's lap, "I had a lot of boyfriends when I was younger, even before Ronnie."

"Yeah?"

"Yeah. I dated a lot, starting in sixth grade when I was with the cool crowd, drinking and smoking and partying all the time. I was a wild girl."

John Huey stroked a greasy snarl of blonde hair. He waited, in vain, for a twitch of jealousy. All he felt was curious.

"Whatta ya mean, a wild girl?"

"Well, you know," she insisted, "a *wild* girl."

"Oh." He didn't know.

She drained the Coke and lit a cigarette. She eyed the TV like a dog drawn to its food dish. John Huey scissor-wrapped her neck between his legs to prolong their discussion.

"Wild girl what?" he shouted in their lovers' baby-talk argot.

She laughed and stuck out her tongue. "Wild girl me!"

"What wild girl me do?"

"Wild girl me fuck wild boy!"

They chuckled briefly. Wanda grew quiet, sulky. John Huey wove her recalcitrant tangles. They lay in silence, listening to distant car door slams and the symphony of neighborhood quarrels.

"They used to sing a song about me." Wanda kissed John Huey's penis through his shorts, then set ear to thigh as if scanning for a pulse.

"The boys sang it in ninth grade, outside my math window during final exams. All the other kids heard it, and even though they were supposed to be totally silent they all laughed, they all looked at me. It was so embarrassing I cried and I wanted to die, but I couldn't leave the room because we were takin' our exam and Mrs. Dalton was there, who was kinda mean, so I couldn't go anyplace." She grabbed a breath. "It was the worst moment of my life."

That was saying something.

"The song went like this." Wanda lay on her back. John Huey thought her eyes were puffing.

> Bang bang Wanda
> Wanda bangs all day
> Who we gonna bang on
> When Wanda goes away
> Wanda had a boyfriend

> His name was Timmy Tucker
> He took her to bed one night
> To see if he could fuck her
> Bang bang Wanda
> Wanda bangs all day
> Who we gonna bang on
> When Wanda goes away?

She hummed one more stanza, eyes fixed on the milky white ceiling.

John Huey took her left hand in his and clasped it, clenched it, enveloped it.

"They sang that song because the day before, five of 'em were up at MacArthur Park behind the baseball stadium and they gang-banged me."

He didn't begin to know how to respond.

"There was John Renner, Robby Schmeichel, Dan Atkinson, Billy Lewis, and Ronnie. They asked me if I wanted to drink with them, that Malt Duck shit we used to drink in high school, and I said OK and went back to the stone pavilion. I had a couple sips, that's all, and John Renner was pullin' at my blouse, tryin' to touch my tits. He was popular, very popular, he was an excellent basketball player, so I let him, then they all came over and before I knew it I was on my back on the cold ledge and they were goin' one after another, bang bang bang, and all the time I was thinkin' how this would make me popular, y'know, make them go out with me, and so I'd hang out with Sue Vallerio and the top, most popular clique of girls. When it was over I threw away my underpants, 'cause they were all wet and I didn't want my ma to find out, and I went home. I was kind of excited the next day, thinkin' about John Renner askin' me out, maybe buyin' me a ring, and before I knew it I heard them singing that song. And then I knew that they were just usin' me, and that I'd never go out with John Renner or the others as long as I lived."

John Huey kissed her forehead, not knowing what else to do.

"Of course, I did end up goin' out with Ronnie—big deal!—so I guess the day wasn't a total waste."

John Huey cleared his throat. "Did Ronnie ever say anything about that afterwards?"

"No way. He acted like it didn't even happen, he never said nothin' about it. And the thing is, once we started goin' out he was insane jealous, always accusin' me of lookin' at other guys or secretly liking his friends or somethin'. And the funny thing is, I already fucked all his friends right in front of his face. So it's not like I was Little Miss Virgin that was so pure and innocent. Jeez, I could never figure him out."

She'd exhausted the subject, or at least wrung it of whatever cathartic or penitential value it had. Lights off and they fell asleep, arms and legs entwined.

"Tell me about Washington. Please?"

They lay in bed, naked, unabashed, utterly comfortable, holding hands loosely, in the soft, contented afterglow of love. A lone white candle glimmered on the nightstand, the flame reflecting off the melting tallow, imbuing the darksome room with a spectral glow. He wondered how any man or woman on God's earth could be unhappy; he wondered if he'd ever feel this way again.

"Huh, John?" She kissed his breast once, twice, curling his chest hairs 'round her index finger. "Please tell me about Washington."

He cleared his throat. To his surprise, his reticence about his former life vanished.

"I blew everything I had," he started. "I don't want to exaggerate, or sound dramatic, but I built myself a good name, did a good business, so to speak, had the world by the short hairs, I guess, and then in one second I blew it all. I tossed it all away."

He stopped to stroke a particularly rebellious knot of Wanda's hair. He kissed her forehead. Then he reclined and continued.

"There's things that'll knock you down, you don't even see coming. And send you crawlin' like a baby back home."

She smiled at the pop music reference. "Bruuuce."

"Yeah," he said absently. "Bruce."

He shut his eyes, quietly replaying and analyzing his professional demise. He remembered David Krull and Jude Nelson and Senator Sean O'Rourke. He tried to imagine just what they thought of him, but he soon abandoned his speculations. Truth to tell, he didn't really care.

Wanda's chin rested above his sternum. She caressed his

shoulders, exaggerating their width and span, much to John Huey's delight. She withdrew her hands when his excitement became manifest—she had questions yet to ask.

"Well, tell me how you blew it. I mean, did you try to, or did you just make a mistake?"

"It was a mistake, I think," he said haltingly. "I had a newspaper column in quite a few papers around the country. I wasn't famous, but I was on the right track. Then I got invited to go on *Face the Nation*, the boring talk show about politics that's on Sunday mornings."

She betrayed no recognition of this anti-Sabbath institution.

"Anyways, I was on the show, debating this black guy about welfare. He was doin' his boring recital of bullshit facts and arguments, and I was doin' mine. He'd say blahblahblah. I'd counter with blahblahblah. He'd cleverly riposte blahblahblah. I'd hit him in the gut with blahblahblah. It was the usual Washington bullshit. Until all of a sudden somethin' came over me. Like a demon or succubus or some evil goddam spirit invaded my body, and before I knew it I said the word 'nigger' on national TV."

He waited for a gasp, a shocked "John Huey, you didn't!" Wanda said nothing. He went on.

"Well, after that I was fucked. All my papers dropped me. My syndicate—the company that distributed my column—dumped me. I looked for other work, but nothin' came up. I realized that with one goddam word I'd slit my throat. I was through. So I decided to come back here, to Batavia, to die."

She accepted his confession, unperturbed, serene, understanding. One thing, however, puzzled her.

"I don't get it totally. I mean, I know about how hard it is to get a new job and everything, and how people screw you over. But why would they do that just 'cause you said nigger? I hear guys say it all the time—I say it sometimes—and I never get fired. Least not for that."

"Well," he stumbled, nonplussed, "I suppose lots of people use that word in normal everyday conversation, but you can't say it on television, at least nonfiction television."

Wanda wasn't getting it.

"It's just something you don't say on TV," he lectured, frustrated by her imperviousness to self-evident facts.

She shrugged, affecting a bored look. It was time to move on to a more pertinent, and beguiling, topic.

"Did you have many girlfriends in Washington?"

"A few," he said, noncommittally.

"How few?" she giggled, pleased at her witticism. Wanda wanted exactitude.

"I don't know," he said, a mite petulantly. "A few. Not too many. A few."

"Did you have sex with them?"

He hated the detour their bedtalk had taken. Swiftly he reconstructed the ancient edifice of lies that served as his public sexual history. When the fabricated pieces fit into place, he smiled the cocksure smile of the ex-roué.

"I may have taken a few liberties with the ladies in my prime," John Huey said, false rakishness invigorating his voice. "Baby, I'm not gonna deny that I pedaled around the block a few times before we met, but that's all water under the bridge. It was a long time ago."

"Who was your first lay?"

"Sheila Morgan," he admitted, not missing a beat. (The name was a portmanteau of his second- and third-grade teachers.)

"How old were you?"

"Seventeen. It was the spring of my senior year in high school"—he stopped, stricken with the terror of the exposed liar: Wanda, unlike his other adult friends, had grown up in Batavia. She'd know where to sniff around, searching for the toothsome but apocryphal Ms. Morgan.

He improvised. "I met her at a bar in Buffalo we used to go to. (Heretofore she'd been a cornfed blonde farm girl.) We danced, kinda hit it off, went back to her place, and. . . ."

He missed the old Sheila Morgan, the voluptuous ingenue he'd bedded in her parents' king-size. He felt a brief pang of guilt for urbanizing Sheila; he hoped the new lie wouldn't erase the teasing image of his fictive paramour, still a hot masturbation property.

"How many times did you sleep with her?"

"Two." Her virtue was relatively intact.

"Did you ever sleep with a girl from Batavia?"

A tough one. With his Washington conquests already established, honesty became the best policy. "Nope," he answered.

"How many girls total, in all the places, have you ever slept with?"

He made a grand show of the counting, squinting his eyes and rubbing his chin and saying, "Uhhhh, let's see, uhhh, yeah, uhhh, hmmmm, uhhh, yup, uh-huh," before divining the sum.

"Eighteen," he said, "not counting you."

She assailed him with a skeptical grin. "C'mon, John, there's no way you slept with eighteen girls, not counting me. You hardly knew what to do the first time we was together."

He protested, feebly. "Whatta you talkin' about? I knew how to do everything, it was *you* I was worried about." But the jig was up, the figleaf removed, he was bare and defenseless, transparent and humiliated. Had he been that inept his first time?

"Look, John. I love you. You make love great. I couldn't ever ask for anything better. But please don't lie to me."

She spoke in stern, measured tones, a scolding. Yet the sting of her reproach abated under the pure, unalloyed affection evident in her eyes.

"I don't care if you were a virgin when we met, just like I don't care if you screwed eighteen girls or eighty girls. I just don't care. All I want is you, and I want you to be honest with me, not lie to me, or think you're better than I am 'cause you lived in a big city and had a big job. I love you, John."

His initial impulse—to avenge the emasculation with a torrent of abuse and vitriol—faded. He lay his head upon her breast, kissed the nipple, and whispered, "I'm sorry, baby, I'm sorry."

She clasped him to her bosom, rocking her lover in the faint glow of the shortening candle.

11

Wanda marched into John Huey's apartment without knocking (he liked that—she was getting comfortable) and made an announcement.

"I am *so* excited."

"What's up, baby?"

"Get me a Genny first. A real cold one. Then I'll tell ya."

John Huey complied; while in the kitchen he heard the flipflapping of Dominique's sneakers herald the little girl's arrival.

John Huey twisted Wanda's beer cap in the privacy of the kitchen, lest the cap prove recalcitrant. He re-entered the living room.

Dominique accosted and hugged him with what John

Huey, against his wishes, deemed a pathetic eagerness. "Hi, princess," he cooed. "Your mommy has some big news for us."

Every fold and crevice on Wanda's durable face creased into a smile. She stood erect, with mock solemnity, assuming the air of a pompous viceroy.

"Attention, please," she proclaimed. "I have an announcement to make. As of next Monday, I, Wanda Morczyck Fay, will no longer be a peon on the line. I'm being promoted to first-shift supervisor and getting a two-dollar-an-hour raise."

At that she threw her arms upward, the touchdown signal, and stamped her feet manically on the floor. Dominique, no doubt perplexed by the substance of her mom's address, nevertheless caught the spirit and did her own little dance, comically hopping around the room doing semaphore signals, a bizarre terpsichorean ritual she'd seen on MTV.

John Huey patted Wanda's shoulder. (He still felt so damn clumsy in the choreography of love.) She grabbed him, he embraced her, pulled her tight, clasping her bosom to his, and he kissed her with pliable mouth. Dominique, fatigued by her brief dithyramb, joined the lovers in tricornered communion, inserting her head just above their now-libidinous groins.

The three remained interlocked for a full five minutes, synergetically, one might say, secure and replenished in their familial triangle, celebrating Wanda's molting of her lumpenskin.

Wanda was sitting at the kitchen table, peeling oranges for her jello salad, tossing the rinds into a red-white-and-blue Buffalo Bills wastebasket. The TV droned in the background.

John Huey returned from his weekly visit to the Richmond Library, pleasantly surprised to find his . . . "girlfriend" is the most apposite noun . . . cooking dinner for him. They kissed, with the peculiarly grave ardor of new lovers. He inspected the potatoes, the jello, the incipient meatloaf, a delightful domestic tableau, before his attention was drawn to a lonely envelope at table's edge.

"Wassis?" John Huey muttered, and his heartbeat accelerated when he noticed the familiar American Foundation logo in the upper left-hand corner. A letter from the Great Beyond—a communication from Hades—a winking, seductive slattern lobbing come-hithers from his erstwhile muck.

He grabbed a Genny and slugged it down, prepping for the mysterious message within. This was no computer-generated junk mail: the envelope bore the half-pressed markings of an oft-used typewriter.

"Wonder who wrote this?" John Huey mused.

He noticed that Wanda had immersed herself in orange peeling, ostentatiously ignoring her man's anxious excitement.

"They're probably kissin' my ass to come back," he jested. "Please, Mr. Ketchum, please come back. Ten thousand Chapel Hill sorority interns miss you."

Wanda threw her knife on the table. It bounced to the

floor. "Just open the goddam motherfuckin' thing, will ya?" she exploded. "You're drivin' me crazy!"

John Huey stood mute. She'd never yelled at him before; did Ronnie have legitimate cause for abandoning her?

"Christ almighty, baby, what's the matter with you? Did something happen today?"

Wanda burst into tears, a spontaneous combustion, drenching the vinyl tablecloth. She covered her face, or most of it, anyway, with her hands.

"Just open the letter."

"Does it have something to do with the letter?" he asked, slow on the uptake. "Did you steam it open or somethin'?"

She would speak no more. The tears stopped as abruptly as they'd commenced, and she walked to the sink to wash the potatoes. When he approached her and tried to plant a kiss on her forehead, she rebuffed him, demanding, "Just open the letter."

Which he did.

It read:

JH:

Down and out in Batavia, my good man? Couldn't you have borrowed the sense and élan to choose a more picturesque site of exile, perhaps Paris or London or Dubuque, for Peter's sake?

I trust you are shining in the local firmament: county arm-wrestling champ, perchance? Or honorable mention in the 4–H most improved sow competition? Really, JH, I understand your hegira—I, too, would lie low, avoiding any sooty fellows, at the event, if I'd intoned a racist imprecation worthy of Theodore Bilbo on le tube de la booboisie. But the dark clouds have passed, chum. I jibe you not. Plenty of employment opportunities beckon to our prodigal son—not least of which may be a prestigious position here in the fusty halls of the venerable (Est. 1977) American Foundation.

Verily, chum, c'est true! You may remember a Mr. Timothy Ripling, he of the epicene gait and bellicose foreign policy. Well, Timothy has left AF, succumbing to the charms of some paragon of muliebrity, and his cushycoo job is open. I made a discreet enquiry last month regarding Mr. Ripling's empty shoes. "Say a candidate for the post appeared," I expatiated, "and he was worthy in every respect: a fine penman, a skilled polemicist, an adept puffster, imbued with a Franklinesque work ethic and rectitude to shame Teresa of Calcutta. Would this fellow be hired?"

"Yes," Vice President Iris J. Fallner responded brightly. "Who is he?"

I revealed your name. Her expression lost its buoyancy at first, I confess, but I saw the lumbering wheels creak in her fund-raiser's mind, and so I tried again.

"Haven't we all sinned?" I asked Ms. Fallner, somewhat sententiously. "Is there one among us who has not sinned? Hasn't God instructed us that self-righteousness is a sin; that forgiveness is divine; that the most debauched will be redeemed, if they but desire it?"

She nodded. I believe she feared that our colloquy was taking a polysyllabic turn that would expose her for the Total Woman whore/charlatan she most arrantly is, so I obligingly switched the subject.

"Ms. Fallner, Mr. Ketchum is a fine writer. He has numerous contacts, an overflowing Rolodex, and a contrite heart. I do not believe that his hiring would hinder our fund-raising efforts, and I beseech you to give this matter some thought." At that I took my leave, a fuddled Iris J. Fallner standing in my wake.

Within the fortnight, she accosted me at the juice-vending machine. "You're right," she admitted cheerfully. "We should hire Ketchum. Sound him out."

Lo, we arrive at this missive's purpose. A job awaits you at the American Foundation, old chum. A fine, sufficiently remunerative job. I hope you will take it—I admit to feeling your absence, acutely.

If you desire, I can hitch up the Pony Express and come to Batavia a-courting, courtesy the bevy of ninety-two-year-old widows whom Fallner sweet-talks into feeding our colossal endowment. Shall I do that? Visit you, around Christmas, say, since Fallner is in no hurry to fill the slot? Shall we loose the dashing and impetuous duo on the easy colleens of Batavia? Write (or call, collect if you wish) and let me know.

Cheers, old chum. You shall return.

Bertram

John Huey replaced the letter on the table.

"Well?" Wanda scalped the potatoes like a vengeful Injun.

"A friend of mine, a guy named Bertram, is comin' to town. Around Christmas."

"And?"

"And what?"

"And why is he coming?" Her voice, denuded of its warmth, tenderness, solicitude, was a simple instrument of communication.

"He's just comin' to see me. And see you. You'll like him, he's a good guy." John Huey tried to imagine Bertram holding court with Wanda. He couldn't.

"Does everyone in Washington miss you? Do the ten thousand girls all miss you?" Sarcasm was not Wanda's forte.

"Well," said John Huey, imperiously, "he's coming to Batavia around Christmas, and we'll have fun, and that's that. How long till we eat?"

"Forty-five minutes," said Wanda, her knife slicing cleanly through the final potato. She washed the scraps down the sink, then stepped into the bathroom to dry her eyes anew.

That night, John Huey took a long walk, stopping in Centennial Park to descry, if he could, the polestar. Three bright points of light vied for the honor.

He weighed the claims of the three pretenders to the North Star throne. They were identical in appearance, at least to the naked eye, and his internal compass could not differentiate among the three. Irresolute, he finally chose his Polaris. "You're it," he grinned at the distant star, and under its stellar influence he put pen to paper and wrote in the dark nighttime park.

BERTRAM:

You know, buddy, a lot of people used to think we were 7th-rate Menckens who couldn't kiss the Sage of Balmer's ass. I inclined to agree, particularly from my new working-class-hero vantage point, but receipt of your letter has changed my mind. I remain a wretch, but you can pucker up to Henry's wizened anus any old time!

Really, Bert, your letter damn near brought weepy tears to my eyes. You're an OK guy. End of mushy part.

I can't believe that ditzy cunt Fallner is warm for my prose form. I met her maybe twice at AF soirees and marveled at her uncanny ability to switch gears from ruthless ramrod martinet to eyelash-flitting sycophant. Her comportment with me fell into the great void between: she oozed some pap about loving my work, then hectored me for not devoting enough columns to SDI or the MX or the B–1 or one those lethal phalluses that make right-wing chicks juicy.

Can she really want me to flack for AF? Me, the Bull Connor of the egghead class? The Kleagle of DuPont Circle? I just can't picture my rehabilitation, buddy. It's not like I'm Khrushchev, airbrushed out of a few photos and snipped out of Russkie encyclopedias but easy enough to reinsert, slate cleaned, into the national discourse. I'm more like Beria—disgraced, selfabhorring, and shot dead. I'm gone, Bert, long, long gone. The mark on my public soul is indelible—you forget that merciful God doesn't pardon us till we're reclined in a pine box, no longer drawing paychecks.

I came to Batavia to die, really. Officially, anyway. I have no future in DC, in politics, in arts or letters or crafts, and I sure as hell didn't want to be a piteous ghost haunting the conservative manse, having jagoffs talk behind my back, wondering, "Why does *he* come here and make us all feel uncomfortable?"

Fuck that life, Bert. Fuck it. Even if I could I don't know that I'd choose public resurrection. "Desolation ain't so bad," wrote Jack Kerouac (yeah, yeah, I sense your gentle smirk—do me one favor and read the guy, OK? He voted Republican, y'know). Desolation in Batavia really ain't so bad either. I walk the byways of the welfare project in which I live, watching the little niggers (I'm already dead, 'member?) toss footballs to each other, listening to the mighty drunken roars of the bearded, emasculated, jobless Cowardly Lions, screaming, "Come here, bitch, don't walk away when I'm talking to you" at their contused wives and girlfriends. I go to Batavia's Richmond Library once a week, a fine old churchly home of the famous books that assholes like Fallner claim to read but also of forgotten novels and manuals and maps and histories and simple descriptions of Batavia and Genesee County and the annihilated Iroquois Confederacy and Mary Jemison and the Angel Moroni and William Morgan and the Anti-Masonic Party and the Erie Canal and Elba and Oakfield and the Baker Gun Works and the 1949 Blue Devils (undefeated in baseball, football, and basketball), and even John Gardner, Putnam Road medievalist, bless his vodka-soaked head. Forgive the rambling, but I'm trying to say that Batavia has a life and pulse and history and memories every bit as strong as DC, the difference being that forests are felled to write about one place and nobody gives a flying fuck about the other. And since I've been banished by the wealthy capital to the shanty boondock—and because I've fallen in love (yes, yes, you'll meet her—I wouldn't know what to say in a letter)—well, I just figure that I'll stick around Batavia for a while.

Would I ever return to DC?

Dunno, Bert.

I can't lie and say that attention and a national forum and picking up perky Connecticut women who drive to aerobics class in Volvos doesn't appeal to me. I'm not a born-again particularist, and I'm not blind to the cruelty and ignorance and frustrated malice that pave Batavia's roads, that infect its social intercourse. The 14-year-olds still make fun of retards, the hicksville jocks still choose the sensitive boys last in gym class, and those bespectacled, innocent, and curious young brainiacs still cry themselves to sleep at night 'cause the average-looking girls with their lockers down the hall don't know they exist. The adults tolerate eccentricity as grudgingly as ever, and intellectual endeavor of even the mildest sort is greeted with hostile suspicion. In Batavia I see, I understand, why thousands/millions/billions/trillions of post-adolescents have fled their hamlets and parishes and towns and prefects and villages for the anonymity of the city. Shit, Bert, that's why I fled.

But the crimes that DC commits reverberate. When Fallner pisses, I get wet. The sins of the provinces, contrariwise, redound only to the hayseeds. My point (well, sort of point) is that DC, and its sister megalopolises, have been picked bone dry. Their aridity—intellectual, spiritual, social—owes to the numberless young weenies, like me, who invade their limits, heedless of permanent contours and stuffing, and live *universal*, rather than regional or local or aboriginal, lives. Hell, when I dwelled in that Potomac hellhole it could've been Boston or Wichita or fucking Rangoon, for all it mattered to me. I learned the vocabulary, I suppose, but never the idiom. I spoke in stilted, formal diction, the language of the tourist. (And I'd argue that that's true for every one of you goddam white-boy sojourners untruthfully puffin' and struttin' and preenin' and prancin' and apparatchikin' yer way thru Washington life. Go home, white man.)

I understand why I fell from grace. It was inevitable, and I'm grateful that it happened sooner rather than later. It'll happen to you, too, Bert, if not in this vale then in the next. Whatever its shortcomings—and I feel each and every one, keenly—Batavia is my home. I move to her rhythms, I float in her currents, her slang is my slang.

You can't transplant people, Bert. You just can't.

You probably think me a fatuous and fraudulent good ole boy, staking claim to a counterfeit heritage. I'm not. Believe me, buddy, I know how prodigiously Batavia sucks. I know that its hierarchy of values, when it comes to the mind, is an inversion of mine. I was born into the wrong place. Tough luck, uh huh. But I've learned in my peregrinations that no grave is more comfortable than the womb; no fight is sweeter than surrender; no path is more pleasurable than the circle; no reward is more satisfying than lying down to sleep at night in my bed in my hometown.

Come visit, Bert. Bring Fallner's offering if you wish. I can't say that it won't be tempting. I can't promise I'll say no. But it'd take one hellacious thunderbolt to raise me from my sarcophagus. It's kinda cozy—no lie, bud.

John Huey

Excerpt From John Huey's Journal

Today I bought a baseball cap.

No big deal; every asshole and his Genesee County brother wears one. Over the last three days I've seen— resting, perching, fitting, alighting, cupping, sitting, and stuck on Batavia heads—hats emblazoned with Wall's Construction . . . Blue Jays . . . Mack . . . Ass, Gas, or Grass, Nobody Rides for Free . . . American Legion Post 62 Batavia NY . . . Kirby's Bait and Tackle Jackson Hole Wyoming . . . Van Halen . . . Syracuse Orangemen . . .

Eastman Kodak . . . Coors . . . Fieldhouse Rte 5 Bushville . . . Starkweather Dodge . . . American Agriculture Movement . . . Corfu Baptist Church . . . Buffalo's Got the Spirit! . . . and the better part of the alphabet, A for Attica, B for Batavia, C for Caledonia, D for Dansville, E for Elba, F for Frewsburg, and so on, each letter a declaration of place, a mark of allegiance to an unknown, unremarkable hamlet containing hundreds, nay thousands, of lives—vital, boisterous, inert, and despairing—that are lived in sin and grace and glory and dejection, all under the watchful benevolent (?) gaze of God, all the while opposed by the grasping institutions that man has constructed in order to dominate his fellow man: the government of the busy, by the bossy, for the bully; the voracious walleye celebretics of the trained media seals; seventy-seven-story midtown Manhattan robber barons to whose ruthlessness cum opulence I used to compose sticky paeans in briefcase days; the literati-culturati, that corrupted clerisy that mistakes the bleating of to-the-manner-born sheep for the robust singing of Whitman's America and that ignorantly confers epitome status on dyspeptic Eastern private school pussies who fuck dispassionately, discuss Levi–Strauss in flash-chic $9 hamburger cafes, and puff dangling cigarettes that will be discarded when they hit their late twenties, the age at which smoking loses its ennui-gloss and slipslides into working-class vulgarity. (Notice the upper-middle-class-produced "Smoking Is Very Glamorous" posters, which use the weathered face of a prole-crone to scare the SAT-conscious Jasons and Jennifers away from the cancer stick.)

So, too, baseball hats.

Wander the thoroughfares of white-boy DC; observe the scurrying pinstriped ants swarming in and out of the squat leviathan slabs of concrete, or the sleek slender elegant glassy modernist deformities wherein deals are made and we poor suckers in Podunk are eyed with all the amorality of the potter contemplating the clay.

> They all perform such useful functions
> From baptism thru extreme unction

I guarantee that you will see not a single baseball hat on a mover/shaker/"intellectual"/bureaucrat head. The ruling class would expose their careful coifs to hailstones the size of Xerox machines before they'd don the national symbol of unaffected localism. Washington's blacks (save the quisling climbers) and the working whites bused in from shabby Prince Georges County, Maryland, are frequently becapped—often identically so. (Redskins, natch.) But you'd sooner see a Negro face at an Academy of Arts and Letters conclave than catch an oligarchic head sweating within an elastic headband.

(For inscrutable reasons, the listless intell-classes of Boston and Manhattan favor regular-guy affectations, commonly the ballcap. How the hardscrabble Maine farmer can stand to root for a Red Sox team that counts so many annoying eggheads among its followers, Lord only knows.)

So.

This morning I walked over to Chuck's Sporting Goods in the Genesee Valley Mall. I could rave on about the array of hats, their splendid iridescence and all that, but fuck it—if I buy the hat for socio-cultural-political reasons, I'm just another Cambridge asshole. Which Chuck may think me already, I suppose.

I was torn 'tween a simple white B on navy (a high-school overrun) and the Buffalo Bills blue bison bisected by red lightning bolt. The Bills design is rather busy and cluttered for my spare tastes, but its garishness won me over. That absurd bison—and the brutal, primitive game the animal represents (baseball is so much more *complex*, and *intricate*, don'cha know, transporting aesthetes like Angell and Giamatti to lyrically cosmic reflections)— convinced me that this was no poseur's hat, this was no dilettante's one-night cruise with a musky sailor; no, this was a final and complete rejection of my outlaw days, that mad epoch in which I'd thrown over the flawed, obscure *men* who begat me—and the matrix that nourished me, albeit not with Stanley Kaplan College Prep succor—and adopted the dress, the manners, the prejudices, the superstitions, the haughty certitudes, the assumptions, the elitism, the hauteur, the hatwear, of mine enemy. The people who shot Huey, who shunned Fred as a stupid janitor, who killed my father in a hail of bullets (those triggers were not pulled by the men carrying the guns, my friends), they're the ones who rule the visible world, and I'd pitched my tent with them.

I'd forgotten that there is an invisible world: invisible, that is, if one's line of sight is coextensive with the tunnel vision of the mass media. There is a world in which Fred exhausts his meager savings buying groceries for the widow next door; a world in which young boys are taught that honesty and kindness ought always to outrank greed, ambition, and power lust; a world in which four men, friendship forged in the daily crucibles of a lifetime's quotidian happenings, grouse around the kitchen table about the injustices inflicted upon them, always remembering that struggle against remote, centralized tyranny is futile and self-defeating. Finally, there is a world in which babies are born and old men die; loves are consummated and marriages are joined; little girls are raised and the sun, outwaiting the clouds, peeks through.

Invisibility ain't so bad. Go, Bills.

12

His army-surplus jacket buttoned to the neck, fur-gloved hands burrowed into his pockets, Bills cap bent forward to deflect the swirling, icy wind, John Huey walked past the iron gates and into St. Theresa's snow-flecked cemetery.

The plots were laid out chronologically and by class: an imposing wall of antebellum grandees and patroons rimmed the perpetually dark, tenebrific cemetery, and even on Batavia's infrequent sunny days their morbid vaults and prideful memorials lay stone cold, shielded from warmth by the eternal and mighty oaks.

Mechanicks, artisans, and farmers occupied the second stratum; their simple markers (CYRUS RONAN BORN MAY 22,

1851 DIED DECEMBER 30, 1899 HE LOVED HIS FAMILY) were not monuments placed carelessly atop the earth, alien and intrusive. Rather, they were of the earth. Time, patience, and the cessation of struggle had harmonized ground and occupant; here, in a small-town boneyard, the fabled state of nature had been realized.

Composing St. Theresa's core were the twentieth-century dead: eighteen-year-old boys whose mangled bodies had been shipped thousands of miles from faraway places — meaningless names on meaningless maps — to be buried under taut, rippling red, white, and blue flags; lonely spinsters who sat in wicker chairs watching the seasons amble by, their vague discomforts and bouts of disquiet soothed (palliated?) by the stern priest and the talismanic rosary; the stolid providers, good ole Jerry/Dave/Bob, who did their best and carved out a fine life for wife and kids — no privation, reasonable happiness — only to be reviled, unbeknownst to them, with supercilious scorn by college-boy art phonies; the town drunks, who discerned early the stacked-deck nature of the game and refused to play the good loser; the white Indians, converts by hook or crook or calculation, granted communion by men who regarded animism as a sin; the athletes dying old, pushing brooms down limitless corridors, the self-generated white heat of shame scorching their vestigial pride and tricking them into exaggerating the gap separating football hero from street-sweeper, which isn't that wide at all; finally the mass of men and women and children whose righteous human conduct caught God's eye, we may pray, but who, to the bedizened, devouring, rewarded idolators of power, lived the unseen lives, listened to the unheard music, died the unmourned deaths.

In this saintly crowd reposed Fred and Richard Huey Ketchum. Though their modest gravestones hadn't been visited in years, John Huey remembered the sectional landmarks (weeping Baby Jesus over the infant Truscott, desecrated cross haunting the heirless miser Woolsey) and located them without much trouble.

The snow flurries had graduated into a squall, and as John Huey approached the family plot, he noticed that he was alone in the cemetery. The blackened gray of the relentless cloudy sky, refracted through the bare, leafless elms, lent the scene an eerie, haunted forest aura, and John Huey had to fight the urge to sputter a hasty benediction and beat a retreat.

The three graves he sought lay contiguous—a little too close, thought the surviving Ketchum, who wondered if erosion and the gradual, imperceptible shifting of the earth might someday unite the trio. Dad's stone, though terse—name, birth date, death date—was the largest, probably because the taxpayers had shelled out for it. At its flowerless base stood an empty flagstaff, which had flown the blue and white colors of New York State for a day or two, long enough for the photomercenaries to take their pictures, before Fred ripped the tiny flag from its holder and tossed it into the nearest trashbin.

To Dad's right was Hazel Ketchum, Grandma, who'd died a quarter-century ago and left a single memory to her grandchild: a handsome, angelic woman in dowdy dress beaming with delight as she let little John Huey turn the cards in her daily game of solitaire.

To Grandma's right was Grandpa, who hadn't a tombstone but rather a humble seven- by seven-inch plaque on which were engraved the vitals of his life: what his name was, when he was born, when he died. A weed encroached upon the marker's lower left-hand corner, and knowing how Fred hated those goddam nuisances, John Huey knelt, carefully uprooted it, and flung it toward the nearby community of Northeast Side deceased mercantilists. Let it strangle Dr. Lee Noonan's kin.

The frozen ground welcomed new snow, a midweek warm spell having denuded it of its white cover. The dirt and grass and weeds were vanishing under the squall's bounty, not to reappear until the long hard winter months had run their course. "Who knows what the world will look like then," John Huey thought to himself, and after a brief spell of self-pity he chuckled, knowing damn well what it would look like. In spring, in summer, in fall, and in winter.

The Ketchum gravesites were so ordinary, so unexceptional, so nondescript. From a height of fifteen feet the names would be indecipherable; from fifty feet the stones would lose their disjunct quality, family and individuals no more; from a hundred feet all the simple markers and unadorned stones would bleed into one vast unified whole, an entity impressive in scope, shapeless and amorphous in character.

Contrast this burial ground with that of the dead's distant

ruler, the storied satrap Rockefeller. He must be entombed in a massive vault, thought John Huey, or perhaps an ancestral pyramid. Bouquets and laurels and tributes from men known to the history books would festoon his crypt; an army of poets no doubt composed florid odes to his rapidly decaying flesh. He supped as a prince in life; he slept as a king in death.

And yet. . . .

Even the most skilled and sedulous publicist could not revivify Attica's dead or cleanse with final absolution the black mark on the Great Man's soul. No mortal possesses such power. And how restive and unhappy must be the wandering wraith of Rocky: his temporal body succumbed just as the light in his eye was being kindled (it is supposed) by the charms of Miss Megan Marshack. Struck dead in a twinkling. His earthly reputation condemned to carry a snickering, ignominious codicil.

Perhaps heaven has an imp after all. Perhaps one needn't wait for a mysterious afterworld to mete out justice. Perhaps men reap what they sow. . . .

Perhaps we mistake fortuity for design. Perhaps Rocky enjoyed the hell out of that final night and died serene, a big shit-eating grin spanning his face.

The wind's velocity had doubled, or trebled, it seemed, and the cemetery was a blizzard of white, trillions of flakes gusting every which way. John Huey felt the cold's sting fading; he knew that numbness followed. His hands were frozen despite the gloves, and it took all his concentration to clench his hands into warmth-seeking fists. It was time to leave.

He painstakingly drew the sign of the cross in the accumulating snow in front of Grandma's grave. "I hope you're happy," he said dumbly, not knowing what else to say. He similarly consecrated a patch of snow in front of his father's tombstone.

"Hi, Dad," he whispered. "You'll be happy to know that Rocky kicked off while he was in the company of a young lovely. He died a laughingstock."

With a minute's effort, John Huey pulled loose the New York flagstaff. "I'll toss it for you. In spring I'll bring a flower to heal that divot."

He began to trace a cross in front of Fred's marker, halting when he recalled the old man's fierce anticlericalism. "Hi, Grandpa," he said, and the thick flakes striking his eyes drew water, tears and snow merging into dozens of confluent rivers winding down his face. "You got a pretty small marker, I guess. Sorry I haven't seen it before. I was too busy being a jerk. I finally came home. Little too late, I guess. Maybe not. I think about you all the time. I've always done that, but I used to do it the wrong way. Make you too much of one thing, or not enough of the other. I think I got you figured now. I'm glad you're here, so close. I live just a couple blocks away. Yeah, in Batavia. I'm home. I kinda think I'll be home for good. I'll see you soon. I love you."

The ground from which the weed had been uprooted minutes ago was blanketed with the gathering snow. John

Huey searched his pockets for some commemorative token to mark Fred's gravesite. He found none. What to do?

An idea seized him. Run home, rummage through the Huey Long/Grandpa file, and select an apposite offering. Place it upon Fred's plaque. Allow the departed a long winter's commune with a kindred soul. Come spring, season of perpetual rebirth, a second Long memento could be sacrificed.

John Huey decided against the plan, not least because the shrill winds and blowing snow made another trip unwise. His benumbed face and portentously tingling toes pleaded for shelter. Besides, what comfort could a stained celluloid pin provide a dead man? Fred knew who he was, he knew what he believed, he did not die confused, confounded by life, uncertain of truth, uncomprehending of evident verities. The Long pin might amuse the deceased and salve the bereaved's conscience, but its real value was exiguous at best. The dead don't need nostalgia.

Better was a message in the snow. Ephemeral, yes; even the most carefully inscribed letters would disappear in the wintry turbulence. And such a natural epistle was the least public gesture one could make. Not a man or woman, not even the most officious and thorough sexton, would ever see it. But Fred would. In the fleeting minutes of the inscription's legibility, Fred would understand, for time immemorial, the immense richness of his bequest. The solid, palpable, unbreakable link between the generations would be clear, once and for all. Nothing would be left unsaid.

In bold, confident letters John Huey's frozen right hand

traced his message into the snow atop Fred Ketchum's long-inhumed body. When he finished, he admired his handiwork for a second or two, then slowly, serenely, he walked out of the cemetery and down the street, to his home. Within ten minutes the scrawled EVERY MAN A KING was filling up with fresh-falling snow. From a height of fifty feet, you couldn't even read the words.

B

Bertram's bus arrived at the station at 7:30 P.M., December 20. He emerged ("alighted" isn't quite appropriate) a minute later, lugging a handsome leather suitcase, jabbering "Thank you, my good man, thank you, my fine fellow" at the bemused bus driver. Buffalo-bound passengers, who remained on the blue and white Greyhound, took the fat dandy's departure as an excuse for joking and merrymaking, and the Christmas season (and Greyhound's punctuality) lent a cheerful, good-natured edge to their jests.

    Bertram dismounted carefully, grappling with each of the three steps as if he were a wary mountain climber negotiating a tricky ledge. His rusticated friend stood next to a City of Batavia trash barrel, gentle white flakes glistening off his baseball hat, shimmering in that magic second before deliquescence.

"Hey, Bertram, lemme help you with that."

"Ah, John Huey, my old friend, we meet again." The two clasped hands, pumping vigorously, and awkwardly considered an embrace, finally deciding against it. John Huey felt the curious stare of thirty-five pairs of bus rider eyes.

"How was the trip?" he asked, relieving Bertram of his luggage.

"Pastoral, shall we say?" replied Bertram, eyebrow arched. For some reason the snow melted slowly upon Bertram's head. John Huey pictured his roly-poly friend after half an hour outdoors, a round twin to the Burl Ives snowman in *Rudolph the Red-Nosed Reindeer*.

He'd watched *Rudolph* two nights earlier with Wanda and Dominique, the ménage à trois twisted into a family curlicue on the couch. 'Nique squealed with delight at Rudolph's flights . . . cried when the misfit toys related their woe . . . found Santa a gruff, distant character who mistreated his elves . . . and at each appearance of the talking snowman was struck dumb with enchantment. Her little eyeslits narrowed, as if regulating the influx of these strange and wonderful images might render them scrutable. When the show ended she announced, "I love Christmas," and she marched off to bed, unbidden, to dream the dreams of children.

"Say, JH, are we hailing a cab?"

Bertram's question—entreaty, really, for Bert hated to walk unless absolutely necessary—was a solecism in Genesee County. One did not "hail a cab"; one called Ace's Taxi and waited until Ace showed up in his Chevy cabriolet, snapping his chewing gum and ceremoniously setting the fare meter at zero. Ace worked maybe four hours a day, mostly carting second-shift workers who'd lost licenses for driving drunk. Plus he had a clientele of perhaps a dozen widows, shoppers all, whom he invariably greeted with an oily "Good morning, Madam, to where can I chaperone you today?" He opened doors, carried bags, and never blasphemed the Lord in front of the widows, and his tips bought him an above-ground swimming pool, much to his wife's pleasure and leisure.

"Yeah, we'll call Ace's Taxi," said John Huey, grudgingly surrendering his vision of Bertram the walking snowman. Ace was there in ten minutes, and the two old friends spent the ride in cautious palaver, Bertram relaying the latest gossip from the American Foundation, John Huey bracing his visitor for the unfamiliar milieu into which he was stepping.

Ace, cursing the speedbumps, deposited his riders at their destination. A decorative wreath—hung minutes ago by Dominique—adorned John Huey's door.

"Your hearth, I presume?" pronounced Bertram, a hint of a smile creasing his lips.

"Yup," said John Huey. "Welcome to Our Town."

Wanda and Dominique were slouched on the couch watching TV. Wanda had warned John Huey that they'd be sleeping over; his protest ("Aw, lemme be alone with my buddy") lacked fire. She was jealous, and he secretly enjoyed it.

"Bert, I want you to meet Wanda, my, uh, cherished

girlfriend, and her daughter Dominique, the most ravishing beauty in John Kennedy Elementary School."

Bertram offered a sweeping bow. He kissed the two popcorn-smelling right hands, but his affections lacked dash. He seemed tired, or perhaps unsure of himself. The absurd confidence that gentry-bred DC women found comic and winsome was curiously absent. Mother and daughter thought the stranger very odd, and not a little creepy.

Sensing the discomfort, an embarrassed Bertram redoubled his efforts. "May I say, Miss Wanda, that you are even lovelier than I had been led to believe?"

She grunted, repudiating the compliment. "She thinks he's making fun of her," John Huey realized, and as the scene dragged out—Bertram's extravagant praises going unaccepted, his simple inquiries ("Are you a lifelong Batavian?") being met with monosyllabic responses, even 'Nique growing taciturn and unfriendly, like any offended mother's daughter—John Huey was reminded just how incompatible his past and present lives were. Not one element—not even his best friend, or the woman he loved—could ever be transplanted from one world into the other.

He wanted to rebuke Wanda for her sullenness, her inability to shift cultural gears and accept pretentious fops as amusing conversationalists, maybe even as friends. He wanted to scold Bertram for his obliviousness to class differences. ("Where did you go to school?" "Batavia." "Oh, have you a school here?" "Of course." "A four-year school?" "Yeah [it dawns on her] . . . oh, you mean college?" "Well, uh . . . [it dawns on him] . . . yes, college, but tell me, uh, was high school a good, ah, experience?") John Huey wanted them to be socially ambidextrous, versatile enough to float in and out of both his lives. He wanted Wanda to ask Bert about Burke and Bert to ask Wanda about Heart. He wanted the three of them to go caroling off into the night, roistering and drinking and gossiping about prose and politics and pussy and pop music. He wanted impossible things, and as Bertram fiddled with the lock on his suitcase the runaway silence that engulfed the room and amplified the drone of the television into a dull roar reminded John Huey that the impossible is impossible.

"Well, I think we're all tired," the host lamely averred, "so maybe we should all get to sleep and have a good day tomorrow."

"Right, oh, right you are, old boy," affirmed Bertram, grabbing at the escape latch. "I fear I've not made quite the impression I'd hoped on your ladies. I pray they'll forgive me and allow me to start anew in the morrow."

Wanda briskly agreed, rousing herself into a fairly chipper "I'm sure we'll get along once we all get a good night's sleep," and she and Dominique went home, *contra* their earlier plans. John Huey walked them to their door, silent mother and befuddled daughter. Wanda kissed her man goodnight, whispered "I hope you're not ashamed of me, lover," and carried her little princess off to bed.

Bertram was profuse with apologies the next day. He ordered a dozen long-stemmed white roses for a 4:30 delivery (for this was a workday and schoolday). The previous night he'd warned John Huey that "a momentous, yea, epochal day will be the morrow," but the coy taunts ended the second his head hit the sleeping-bag pillow. At a Perkins Restaurant ham-and-eggs breakfast, he resumed the tease.

"Yes, old fellow," he said, stuffing a grossly buttered biscuit into his maw, "years from now I imagine you'll look back on today as a watershed. As an abrupt and uplifting pivot. As every bit as important as the day your sire assured his blushing date, 'Don't worry, these things are leakproof.'" Bertram roared at his rare sortie into bawdy humor, and all Perkins' eyes fixed upon him, whereupon he belched shards of biscuit onto his plate.

"Yech," spat an old lady at an adjacent table.

John Huey had to laugh, and did, but before he could ascertain whether his friend was at all abashed by that public eructation Bert demanded, in hushed tones, a vital bit of information.

"What with all your recent ignominy, and your quite inexplicable Batavia exile, you must have hit several new nadirs. Points at which you sat ground zero in the primeval abyss. Moments of grief and self-hatred that no human being has ever imagined, much less experienced. What I want to know, old fellow, is the location of your most sorrowful epiphany—the spot where you spent your worst second on earth."

Bertram grinned, but he was not joking. He wanted to know.

"Hard to say, buddy," drawled John Huey. "Probably at the pavilions up behind the high school, where I helped a couple Iranians gang-bang your grandmother."

Bertram snorted. "Just the sort of lame jape I'd expect from a Bedouin in this intellectual Sahara. Now listen, crude fellow, I'm quite serious. Where did you hit bottom?"

"Jeez, Bert, what the fuck do you wanna know this stuff for? I never hit bottom. I'm OK. Really. I understand Batavia, you know, and I kinda like it."

"Must I repeat myself, oh obdurate one?" sighed the corpulent dandy. John Huey noticed that Bertram twirled his coffee cup with his left pinkie; he wondered if it took much practice.

"Oh all right, for Christ's sake. I don't know what kind of prank you have in store, but I'd say my worst moment in Batavia happened when I was takin' a walk around town and I stood in front of this girl named Linda Hunnage's old house. I used to make wicked fun of her, she must've been the saddest trash-waif in a world of Mundt Avenues, and I stood there and realized that I'd committed evil acts and that there might not be any way to atone for them. I wasn't sure. I'd say that was the worst thing—feeling like a wretched jerk and having no idea what to do with that fact."

"Fine." Bertram slammed his palms on the Formica tabletop. "To Hunnage's house we go!"

They walked the eight or ten blocks, John Huey astonished at his sedentary pal's new vigor. Bertram never even broke a sweat; the rush of anticipatory energy kept his flubbery legs churning and churning, till his gait had something approaching momentum. "My friend, have I a surprise for you," he promised every minute or two, with so thorough a simper that his face looked like a grotesque Mardi Gras mask.

Hunnage's house was dressed in snow. A wreath was stuck on the storm door's plastic pane. There was no sign of the tenacious vine clinging to the eavestrough. Whether it was hibernating or finally dead, one couldn't tell. Spring held the answer, and she would take her sweet time divulging it.

"So this is the House Beautiful?" croaked Bertram, arms folded, a contented lord. "This is the place?"

"Yup." John Huey felt foolish inspecting a residence in broad daylight. He leaned against a NO PARKING THIS SIDE OF STREET 9 AM TO 2 PM sign, hoping that the neighbors would think him a surly teenager and pay him no mind. "Well, let's get to the point, Bert," he said impatiently.

"Ah, yes, the point." Bertram stepped lightly to John Huey's side. "The point, my good man, is that you're being recalled from Coventry. The Scarlet Letter is being erased. A wailing Jesus is being taken down from the cross and led to a feast with Pilate. To dispense with metaphor and put it into the Genesee County vulgate, you're off the hook. You're clean. Rehabilitated. Buffed and waxed and rubbed and polished to a shinier finish than you ever dreamed of. You, old chum, are born again."

John Huey was tantalized. Seduced. He tried to subdue the rising excitement inside. "What the fuck are you talking about?"

"This. You recall my little chat with the Goddess Fallner, related so entertainingly in my recent epistle?"

"Yeah."

"Well, we spoke again. And again. And again. She's a religious woman, John Huey. She believes in prayer and sacred heart and supplication and the forgiveness of sin, particularly when it redounds to the financial benefit of the American Foundation. Which, in your case, it does. You see, Fallner and the Foundation have been begging a, shall we say, amply endowed and venerable philanthropic organization for years, always being turned down in polite but firm terms. Fallner thinks the rejection owes to the philanthropy's liberal slant, which is probably true, but she keeps panhandling year after year because she's convinced that right-wing money is drying up and the Foundation's future depends upon an infusion of, quote, nonpartisan, endquote, alms. Well, this year Fallner hit upon a new scam. She thinks that liberals go limp when confronted with anything smacking of race—they'll shell out trillions to soothe their consciences, just so long as Negro toughs don't bully them on the street. Her proposal was this: launch a Foundation project to be called—get this—'Black and White Together'—whose mission is to, quote, promote cooperation among the races, laying the groundwork for a society without racism, filled with the spirit of goodwill and brotherhood, endquote. The kicker is this—the codirectors of this praiseworthy project would be Mr. Tommy Jackson, erstwhile Black Panther and assaulter of Caucasians, and Mr. John Huey Ketchum, the columnist who has courageously overcome his racism and now intends to devote his life to blood-mixing and miscegenation. You, sir, Mr. Co-Director, are in line to receive a two-hundred-thousand-dollar grant and an image reconstruction by a battalion of DC's most skilled flacks. Welcome back to the world, John Huey."

The regenerate racist muttered, "Uh, thanks," spitting at the base of the No Parking sign. His head was awash in a sea of reactions: vindication, pleasure, cynicism, hope, anticipation, but mostly, spreading in dense annulated circles from the pit of his stomach, the dread knowledge that the price of Fallner's ticket to redemption was the desertion of Wanda. The god utilitarianism was demanding a sacrifice: either deny DC's offer of professional salvation, or renounce the sum of his Batavia experience. To John Huey's shame, the choice cloaked itself in uncertainty.

"Uh, I don't know Bert, I don't think . . . I can't do it. It's just too weird."

"Oh, come now," his friend admonished, "the decision you must make is obvious to the blindest eye and densest brain. You can't very well stay here: you've *outgrown* this place. It may be quaint; you may invest it with a modicum of bucolic charm; but *it's an intellectual desert,* for goodness sake. Who will you talk to for the rest of your life? The milkman? 'Yes, Bucky, leave two quarts of skim tomorrow. Say, have you read much Gaddis?' Come *on,* good man. This town has nothing for you. Nothing. Now, I'm sure your amatory interest Wanda is a fine woman of sterling character, but *what will you talk about?* Her foreman's churlishness? Come, my good fellow, your relationship is a mésalliance of the first order. It *can't last*. DC, by contrast, admitting its sundry shortcomings, is your *home*. It offers intellectual and social succor and nourishment. It offers entertainment. It offers women who know how to read. *That* is your place. In *our* community. Working for the Foundation at a generous salary, with a higher profile than before, with the world your beat. Please come back, JH. We need you. I need you."

The friends said nothing more. They walked back to Cardboard City in silence, punctuated by Bertram's boots crunching the icy snow underfoot.

"Time for a nap," Bertram announced as they entered Apartment 132. "Wake me at dinner time."

John Huey agreed. Before his visitor fell asleep, he promised to have an answer for him by morning.

The second night repeated the first. Wanda, plainly uncomfortable with Bertram's presence, was sullen and withdrawn. (She did thank him for the flowers, though.) Dominique behaved better—Bert complimented her manners, which drew a shy smile—but she seemed uncharacteristically inert. No jumping, no dancing, no aping of her favorite MTV moves.

Bertram was a pale imitation of himself. The poor fellow tried hard to shed his more flamboyant affectations, even spicing his conversation with a slang word or two ("hot-diggety" stuck out), but the expurgated Bertram was wan and unnatural. He made an early reference to Albert Jay

Nock; how painful it was to see the neo-Nockian quickly erase his tracks with a half-hearted "But Nock was a boring chap, really, and we needn't waste time discussing him."

Dinner broke up early, and John Huey announced that he would be sleeping at Wanda's because they had "some things to talk over."

"Yes, by all means, leave," encouraged Bertram. "I shall be interested in the outcome of your pillow talk." All were in bed by 10:00 P.M.

For Wanda, the undressing had a dreamy, trancelike quality. As she slipped out of her pants and into her teddy, her mind seemed to sever from her body and hover above the bed, dispassionately critiquing the lovers' bodies. (She: too skinny, meager breasts, that hair! He: creeping paunch, steep nose, dulling eyes.) The idea that this was their last night together and that she'd better do something fast nagged at her so persistently that she became inured to it, accepting of it. She'd picked his world up off the ground; her work, apparently, was done.

They lay in the black stillness, uncomfortable, trembling, until she spoke, softly. "Are you leaving Batavia?"

"Never, my love," he longed to answer, but gallantry failed him.

"Uh, I just don't know. Bertram offered me a job, a fantastic job, really, and I told him I'd think about it. So I'm thinkin' about it."

"What are you thinking?"

"That if I go, things will be like before, and if I don't they'll be like they are now."

"What are they like now?"

"Well, I live in the place where I was born, near my family's graves, and I'm crazy in love with a woman who saved me, and her beautiful daughter."

John Huey expected Wanda to burst into tears at that, but she didn't. She continued her questioning in cool, logical voice.

"What were they like before?"

"I lived in a big city with a good job and people heard of me."

"Were you happy?"

"Kind of."

"Are you happy now?"

"Yes."

"Are you in love?"

"Yes."

"Were you in love before?"

"No."

"Then I don't see why you want to leave."

"I didn't say I wanna leave. I don't. I found what I wanted, what I never had, what I had and lost, all here. I want to stay. But I can't live some kind of idyllic rural-hick life, hangin' out at the feedstore all day. I gotta have money. *We* gotta have money. My savings are just about out. Gone. Depleted. I gotta get a job. And I just think that stockin' shelves for some asshole ex-jock manager all day would drive me outta my mind. So I don't know what to do."

He grasped her hand. She squeezed back. She threw her left leg over his hips and mounted him, her groin pushed against his. She sat above him, straddling him. He became excited.

"I'll tell you what," she said playfully, buoyed with sudden confidence. "At work we need to hire two new sweepers. I got a big say in the hiring. I can pull a few strings." Her smile stretched to an impossible breadth. "I can get you in there if you want. It may not be much to a big TV star—four bucks an hour. But you're smarter than any of the guys there, and you'll get promoted and advanced in no time flat. Probably end up bein' my boss. But first," she said, rocking on him with mischievous ferocity, "I get to be yours. Whatta you say?"

Their rocking became synchronized, she thrusting her pudendum at him, he rubbing her with erect penis. With each movement their grimaces tightened, until in one glorious moment the sky opened, the earth quaked, the rains came, and with the deep and plangent voice of a thousand generations of Ketchums John Huey bellowed, "Yes Yes Yes."

———

John Huey stood with Bertram outside the Batavia Greyhound Bus Station, soft flakes of snow kissing their foreheads, then dissolving into rivulets trickling down frozen cheeks.

"Well, old man," harrumphed Bertram, "I suppose you're a Batavian now and forever. I suppose you shan't be returning to the District."

"No, I s'pose not."

"You will make an honest woman out of your delightful concubine Wanda, *oui*?"

John Huey laughed; Bertram had yet to shed his trifling French pretensions. He thought to call him "Anglophile manqué," but let it drop.

"Yeah, I'll ask her, we'll probably be married in the spring, if I ever get up the guts to pop the question. I'd like to adopt Dominique, but. . . ."

"Yes, yes, the working-class cult of the paterfamilias. I expect her brutish father is loath to cede official custody."

"Yeah, I expect so." John Huey arced a sleek spit missile into a nearby moraine. "It don't really matter, though. I'll still raise her. There's still time to strike that template with my own image. She'll be my . . . my . . . prepubescent palimpsest."

The bus that was to bear Bertram out of Genesee County pulled into the station. A voice, distorted by amplification, announced its imminent boarding.

"You'll send me galleys of the Burke book, right?"

"Certainly I will, certainly, certainly," assured Bertram. "My schedule has been retarded by . . . unexpected problems of a personal nature, but once Logos reintroduces herself I shall satisfy her without delay."

"Good, good. And you'll let me know when you give up the bachelor's life?"

"Well . . . let's just say that not all men are blessed with a Wanda Madonna. We loveless fellows have endured sexual privation for centuries, you know, so I can't promise deliverance overnight."

Bertram: obese, a thirty-year-old virgin, clad in clinging '40s suitjacket and absurd string tie, four Nestles' Crunch bars bulging from his hanky pocket, picked up his leather suitcase and prepared to embark.

The two friends shook wet hands.

"Goodbye, JH. Godspeed."

"Bye, Bert. Write me."

As Bertram ascended, laboriously, the three steps into the bus, he turned and called to his companion. "Are you still writing, old buddy?"

John Huey shook his head no. Punditry would have to survive without him.

Upon second thought, an unfinished essay presented itself. "Wait, Bert," he called. "Gimme your bus schedule and a pen."

Bertram obliged; the five or six boarders behind him grumbled.

John Huey scribbled a note on the schedule and pressed it into his friend's hand. "It's my reformulation of Ketchumist principles," he said, and Bertram, puzzled, accepted it and disappeared into the Greyhound.

The bus crawled out of the station's circular drive and rumbled down Main Street, stopping at the multiple red lights the city fathers had installed in the heady boom days of the distant past.

Bertram watched the white-peaked town inch by. He saw the stately mansions of Batavia's early lairds; the abandoned shoe factory, smokeless and dead; the red neon Super Duper Grocery sign; a staggering drunk veering through hip-deep snow; two little girls making angels in the lot adjoining Cardboard City; a lone wreath taped to the burnt-oak door of the Seventh Day Adventist church; hurried gift-buyers swarming into the K–Mart Plaza parking lot; a lanky teenager hurling an icy snowball at a passing car; leafless maples patiently awaiting spring; a muffled woman, parka-snug, shoveling a long driveway; a husky romping in the snow with a happy towhead boy; a solitary blackbird perched atop a telephone line; and he saw a snow-quieted cemetery, preternaturally calm, containing all the generations that had ever been born, and lived, and died in a neglected town tucked away at the western edge of what historians used to call the Burned–Over District. The cemetery was bounded by an ever-opened gate; no impassable barrier separated the dead Huey Long men and the dead prison guards from their flesh-and-blood lineage walking the tree-lined streets. Living and dead were quartered on the same few acres, so that when life gave way to death one didn't have to move all that far.

Town melted into country, and Bertram unfolded the inscribed schedule that John Huey had handed him. Beneath the Genesee Local's itinerary was scrawled John Huey's manifesto:

Politics is the assassin of the soul

Bertram smiled, stuffed the declaration into his pocket, and pressed his face against the window, watching farms and fields and frozen creeks rush by. The bus hurtled on to Washington.

14

On the first day of spring in a dark factory men's room, while scrubbing in desultory manner a row of fetid white urinals, John Huey Ketchum, janitor, sang softly aloud a bawdy roundelay of sexual misconduct, verse that was in no way consonant with Burke's admonitions to humility.

John Huey's janitorial duties, as junior member of the Consolidated Packaging Inc. maintenance team, were none too taxing: he rode from bathroom to bathroom in a converted orange golf cart. He swept the floors in each lavatory, scrubbing the toilets, replacing the coarse hand towels, refilling the pink lotion, refilling the rag box, and joking with the other workers, some serene and satisfied with their bounty, some juiced with blind hate, forever clawing.

His colleagues (save Wanda, whom he seldom saw during work hours) had no inkling of his past. He no longer answered "Washington" on those infrequent occasions when someone asked, "Where are you from?" Instead, he said, fluently: "Batavia."

He got a kick out of the older janitors, with their blithe uncouthness in speech and dress. His favorite janitor joke, a staple of the trade, went:

JOHN HUEY: Excuse me, sir, but would you happen to know anything about history?

FOIL: Uh, yeah, sure, I guess I do.

JOHN HUEY: Good. Because I'm a janitor, and while I was sweeping the floor in the ladies' room I found this here Granny Rag. I was wondering if you could tell me what period it's from?

If you heard him tell it, in the cool dampness of the factory john, you would laugh.

On this spring day, when not serenading the toilets, John Huey scribbled with a pencil stub upon a taut sheet of beige paper towel. He was writing a letter to Bertram Moost, full of thoughts that visited him in the dim stalls. His parchment read:

BERT:

I lied to you about not writing any more. I'm a poetaster and half-assed essayist and will be till the day I die. I fear, however, that my gimlet eye has blurred and refocused, and from the improbable vantage point of white-trash Batavia my view grows more eccentric by the second. I sometimes feel like a lonely kid bouncing a rubber baseball off a brick wall: the grounders come back, but they bounce in slow irregular nonpatterns. So it is with my thoughts: alone, without intellectual comradeship (or the strictures that go with institutional affiliation), I fling my cerebrations against invisible walls, and the grounders I catch are unlike any I've seen at the ballpark.

In this aspect—and this aspect alone—Wanda provides no sustenance. I'll be catching slow, bad-hop grounders for the rest of my life. I thank the Lawdy, buddy, that you will always listen. And riposte weakly weekly.

With trepidation, then, I offer this gobbet of diseased flesh, composed during the intervals between shithouse sweepings. If it sounds inauthentic, or peevish, just toss it in the trash, and sooner or later a colored helot like me will empty it into a capacious garbage bin.

NOTES FROM THE FINISHING LINE MEN'S ROOM

Most writers, artists, and musicians at some point in their young lives think that their *talents*, in addition to their ambitions, outstrip their provincial little hometowns. They are restive, and unsatisfied, and ought to leave, soon.

A few will become successful in the remote, glittery metropolis and will view themselves as lucky refugees from boortown. Witness Buffalo-bred Michael Bennett, the choreographer venerated in Manhattan, ridiculing his hometown as synonymous with suicide.

Others will leave home for good, at least artistically. Their native soil will be absent from their hearts and their work, and they will accept rootlessness as their lot. As did Lockport's Joyce Carol Oates, who is not called Daughter of the Barge Canal for good reason.

A few of us leave our homes and discover, years and miles later, that sense of place that heretofore lay dormant. If we remain distant from our source we become vaporous sentimentalizers at worst, loving and elegiac poets if we're lucky. Few of the Southern Agrarians lived in Dixieland when *I'll Take My Stand* was published, and literature is not the worse for it. Carl Carmer, on the other hand, traded the muggy starry nights of Alabama for the chill evenings and reluctant hills of his beloved upper York State: readers may judge if the prodigal son honored—and was honored—by his return.

Finally, there are the rove-nots. The inspired youth who never leaves home may be discerning enough to understand his region without benefit of peregrination: if so, he is that rarest avatar, a poet of the people, and he is worthy of idolatrous affection. Likelier, the sedentary, unhappy youth will become a smug and petulant member of the local literati manqué, a pathetic and supercilious jerk who scorns his neighbors and mindlessly apes the fashions and prejudices of that distant capital he never had guts enough to invade.

Lord Acton, oft quoted and never read, said that exile

is the nursery of nationalism. And how sweet must be the triumphant train ride home for the welcomed expatriate. But there is a price to pay. . . .

"Whatcha writin', Ketchum, you hunk a' shit?"

John Huey folded the letter and stuffed it into his workshirt. He faced Tony Sinotti, first-shift maintenance foreman.

"Ah, nothin' really, just a note thanking your grandmother for last night."

"Fuck you, pencil-dick," the foreman replied, and the two men spat out jocose obscenities for a good five minutes, after which they speculated on the outcome of the impending college basketball championship game. Tony hadn't the bullying tendencies of the other foremen, who were liable to write you up for cracking wise. Lèse majesté was no more decriminalized here than in Washington.

"Say, are you and Wanda still plannin' to move outta Cardboard City?"

"Yeah, soon as we find a decent place."

"Well, listen, friend of mine told me that some bag out in Elba is renting a few shacks. Pretty cheap, he says, and not so dirty a lazy shit like you couldn't clean 'em out."

"Thanks for the tip," said John Huey, genuinely pleased by Sinotti's small act of kindness.

When he saw Tony that afternoon in the break room, John Huey bought his Sicilian boss a bag of oily potato chips out of the vending machine.

"Thanks, asshole," said the foreman. "Hey, you got a ticket on the Lottery tonight? They're givin' away forty fuckin' million dollars."

"Nah, I ain't much on that Lottery shit. Big waste of money, that's all it is."

"Yeah, but forty million clams? Somebody's got to win it."

"I guess," replied the janitor Ketchum. "But it just seems stupid to try. I wouldn't be a rich bastard if you paid me."

Sinotti snickered at that remark—easy for a shithouse sweeper to act the noble soul, untouched by filthy money!—and he walked away, appetite dulled by the greasy fare that had salted his gullet.

Quite by accident John Huey found himself standing at the intersection of Market and Main Streets in the tiny commercial district of Attica.

An imperious besuited manager of ConPack, a mustachioed Buffalo Italian who never tired of mentioning his "college degree in business from the university," had drafted John Huey to run an errand that required his presence in "a real hillbilly asshole place" for an hour or two.

"Okay," responded John Huey to the boss's demand, and after a ten-minute drive down Route 98 in the Italian's Cadillac, the village of Attica unfurled before John Huey's eyes, exactly as it had appeared almost two decades before.

Market Street consisted of the same unprepossessing paint stores and insurance offices and superettes and bars, bars, always bars, never quite slaking the nagging thirsts of the prison guards and cooks and would-be prison guards and cooks who swarmed into the gin joints at every shift change.

He parked the car on Main Street, directly above the opaque green waters of the Tonawanda Creek, calm and unruffled and turbid with sewage, as always. He tossed a pebble into the creek, and it disappeared without a ripple.

Tucked in between a video emporium and a vacant storefront was a crumbling sandstone Masonic Temple built, so it said, in MDCCCCVII, or seven decades after the Anti–Masonic fever had run its course. John Huey wondered, for one silly second, if Anti–Masons existed still, furtively plotting the demise of the Satanic order. In the Burned–Over heyday, an Attican named Ebenezer Mead had written with millenarian finality: "The Lord rides upon the whirlwind and directs the storm." Could an ordinary mortal, let alone the Lord, find transport in the zephyrs that blew softly about modern Attica?

John Huey completed his assigned task in a matter of minutes. He walked back to his car, ConPack-bound parcel in hand, stopping every few feet to admire the stately Victorian houses of Main Street, home to Wyoming County's nineteenth-century grandees.

In no hurry to return to his sweeper, John Huey stepped into Lucy and Hugo's Attica Inn for a quick beer. The bar, nearly empty at 1:30, would fill to bursting in another hour and a half, when the first shift ended at the prison.

Strangely, in this company town, symbols and references to Attica's lifeblood were absent from the bar. No glossies of sharpshooters perched in prison towers speckled the wall, no crude hand-painted signs contained aphoristic comment about the daily horrors of Cell Block D, not even a grainy photo of guards ebullient with barroom camaraderie was to be seen. Lucy and Hugo's was a sanctum sanctorum, a refuge inviolate, a place to imbibe and relax, out of the long shadow of the gray behemoth on Exchange Street, taker and giver of life in a village whose residents paid with every breath for the covenant that made them the devil's jailers.

On the jukebox, a multimillionaire country and western singer was growling a threnody about "losin' my job at the factory." The bartender was an Indian, with hatchet nose and slick black hair too short to cover a bulging forehead scar. Men, bearded, hirsute, sat dolefully at the bar, eyes translucent from diurnal boozings.

The bartender nodded at the new patron. "Yeah, can I get a Genny?" asked John Huey.

Three stools down, a bearish young man in frayed leather jacket awoke from alcoholic stupor. He stared at John Huey, who nervously feigned interest in the cocktail napkins.

"Whaddja wan, ya asssh-hole?"

The bestirred man tried to spit; the expectoration caught in his beard, giving it a roan appearance.

John Huey cleared his throat and tried to read the label on a far-off whiskey bottle in the vain hope that his truculent bar-fellow would sway back into unconsciousness.

"I shed, whaddja wan muthafucker fuckhead faggot?"

The man, relishing the crisp pronunciation of each obscene f, staggered off his barstool, primed for battle. As John Huey braced himself for the inevitable sloppy fight, a deus ex machina clad in a Property of Attica Correctional Facility sweatshirt intervened, guiding the alcoholic back to his stool, soothing him with, "Sit down, man, come on, sit down, he didn't do nothin' to ya. Just sit down and be cool and we'll have another beer. Just be cool about it."

"I wan him. I wan him. I wan him, goddam it." The reprobate's threats were losing their urgency, as if thirty seconds of inchoate fury had depleted his meager reservoir of vigor. The man seemed to realize this as he steadied himself on his stool.

"Just sit down, man, just sit down. He didn't do nothin', you've just had too much to drink, buddy. Just sit back and cool it."

The intercessor turned to John Huey. "I'm sorry, man. He's not really a bad guy. He's just had a couplathree too many."

"It's cool," responded John Huey, meekly. "I gotta go anyway."

He chugged his beer, wiped his mouth with his shirtsleeve in a lame attempt at manly swagger, and walked toward the door.

"Yeah, thash right, you pussy," hollered the drunk. "Walk outta here, you faggot. You don' belong here, your ass don' belong here, get the fuck outta here, you faggot. Go back to where you came from."

Back on Market Street, John Huey breathed an emancipatory sigh of relief. He walked briskly to the car, gunned the engine, and sped north on Route 98, flipping on the radio once he passed the Attica town line and crossed into the friendlier confines of Alexander. The thought of visiting the prison never occurred to him.

15

In early April, the snow clouds finally conceding defeat, Wanda and 'Nique and John Huey moved out of Cardboard City and into a peeled-paint one-story dwelling in the northwestern Genesee County town of Elba (an address that gave Bertram no small pleasure).

Their new home—or shack—sat at the end of a long, rambling dirt road, amidst acres of the loamy, superbly fertile Genesee soil that the agronomists call muck. Half a mile up the road lived the sixth-generation farmer who tended this particular plot of muck; out back, a settlement of shanties awaited the incoming migrant workers, whose sunny months were spent educing potatoes and onions from the rich black dirt.

A crusty neighbor warned John Huey and Wanda that their homestead, with its corroded floor tile and leaky roof and insect lair, was "not fit for wolves nor wild dogs nor even a migrant." They thanked him for his counsel and moved in anyway. Wanda had insisted that they "get the hell out of Cardboard City, as soon as possible." Her partner agreed. Summer loomed, and John Huey did not want the speed-bumps to form a permanent hindrance in 'Nique's mental and cultural landscape. In Elba, his daughter-in-all-but-law could walk freely.

Their second day in Elba was also 'Nique's ninth birthday. En route to dinner, the trio drove through the vernal brilliance of Genesee County, land bedecked in renascent greens. 'Nique identified the trees along the roadside, shouting "A poplar! A poplar!" at everything from a weeping willow to a white birch.

They ate at the Chess King, mecca of down-on-their-luck Genesee gastronomes. 'Nique ordered a beef on *weck*, Western New York's sturdiest delicacy, and after dinner she was presented with a softball mitt and a book of poems by Elizabeth Madox Roberts. She seemed pleased.

That night, John Huey led his lifemates on a tour of time-worn landmarks. They visited the white limestone church in Caledonia that served as a way station on the Underground Railroad. They visited the church in Warsaw (it shall ever stand!) that was the site of the first Liberty Party Convention, in 1839. They visited John Gardner's boyhood farm on the Putnam Road, which John Huey consecrated with a shot or two of vodka for that thirsty and deserving soul; he pledged that on his next visit, he'd deliver a toast in Old English.

They walked along the Putnam Road shoulder in the dimming gloam, 'Nique, Wanda, and John Huey, holding hands in rapturous silence. When they stopped to inspect an abandoned farmhouse, John Huey bent over and kissed 'Nique on the forehead, whispering, "I love you, little angel." Then he turned to her mother. Wanda's flaxen hair, knotty and refractory still, mirrored the distant light of the gibbous moon. Wanda, gorgeous Wanda, had endured hardships far more arduous than he; it is much easier, he knew, to find grace in a fall than to achieve it in workaday life. She was powerful and resilient, and a man who had made profit off of words found it difficult to understand the complex language of her actions—so difficult that he wanted to spend all of his days trying.

He kissed her, and she him, and he said, effortlessly, "Wanda, will you marry me?"

She said yes, yes she would, and she held him with the certainty of the ages.

They made one last trip that night, under the infinite expanse of the midnight sky, the waxing moon blessing with fulgent beams every house and acre in the county. They visited the cemetery, and in that necropolis, teeming with Burned–Over specters luminous with disappointment in their children's lethargy, they prayed over three unremarkable graves, and with that scorched-earth benediction the family was finally and fully inspirited with the Holy and Avenging Ghost that had always been their Burned–Over birthright.

EVERY MAN A KING

EXCERPT FROM JOHN HUEY'S JOURNAL

I still read the Sunday *New York Times*, and if I skip "Bulgarian Minister Addresses Parley," and A. M. Rosenthal's weekly secretions, I compensate by poring over the outrageously elitist and off-limits WASPy warren known as the Wedding Pages.

I used to read the *NYT* religiously—well, avidly—when I toiled for the dipso O'Rourke, though I surrendered my naive faith in a free, adversary press after seeing one too many *Times*man rewrite an O'Rourke press release as news or paint a hagiographic portrait of Senator Sean just because the sod flattered the newsboy with a phone call or a private drink in his sacristy. Whatever line once separated state from press has long been erased; indeed, the chief reason I still plunk down two bits for the rag is to witness the servility, the toadying to the powerful, the squalid sycophancy to the rich and famous that unborn historians will mistake for the Zeitgeist of our era.

This past Sunday I came upon the peak, the apotheosis, the sublime crystallization of all that I have come to hate. Rage, alas, is futile; the offending sentence is as representative—and as common—as a clump of dirt is to the earth.

The *Times Book Review* carried an essay by one Jason Lindsay, who, in the course of pretentiously twaddling about some abstruse thing or other, referred to the "rural bleakness and cultural blankness of Western New York, an intellectually barren region with cheap land, open skies, and houses that are virtual shrines to the decorative genius of Montgomery Ward and Sears Roebuck."

That's where I grew up, asshole. And so did a lot of other boys and girls who weren't born with silver thermometers up their rectums. Recti. Maybe we wear CAT hats and haven't seen the O'Keeffe exhibit at the Met, but we got more red blood in one fingernail than you do in your whole scrawny Fire Island-Martha's Vineyard-Hamptons–tanned body.

The flannel-shirted Genesee County bohunk whose pickup just passed your Volvo on the Thruway knows exactly what you think of him and his Monkey Ward's end table and his wife's JC Penney jeans and his kid's Buffalo Bills football poster. He knows, Jason, he knows, and come the day the stool is kicked, the tinderbox lit, and the wire tripped, your M.F.A. and *Review of Books* sub and all the guilty green in your psychiatrist daddy's trust fund ain't gonna save your pale ass from the whippin' it's deserved since the Dawn of Time, when the handsomest Cro–Magnon snubbed the plug-ugly Neanderthal janitor.

Jason, I want you to read what Walt Whitman, American, wrote in the days before this country had such an enormous syphilitic dick up its asshole:

When I pass to and fro, different latitudes, different seasons, beholding the great crowds of the great cities, New York, Boston, Philadelphia, Cincinnati, Chicago, St. Louis, San Francisco, New Orleans, Baltimore—when I mix with these interminable swarms of alert, turbulent, good-natured, independent citizens, mechanicks, clerks, young persons—at the idea of this mass of men, so fresh and free, so loving and so proud, a singular awe falls upon me. I feel, with dejection and amazement, that among our geniuses and talented writers or speakers, few or none have really spoken to this people, created a single image-making work for them, or absorb'd the central spirit and the idiosyncrasies which are theirs— and which, thus, in highest ranges, so far remain entirely uncelebrated, unexpress'd.

Are the delicate boys who paint in lofts and the granny-glass'd girls who line up to watch adaptations of E. M. Forster novels "alert, turbulent, good-natured, independent"? Is there anything in your life, anything at all, at which Whitman would not have retched?

You belittle Monkey Ward's and shrink from conversation with black men and ridicule fat girls and depict Atticans as benighted rednecks and hang up on phone solicitors and call our homes "rural bleakness" and think the martyred Huey Long was an uppity cracker.

For the living there is scorn and mockery and derision and tyranny; for the dead, sanitization and posthumous honor. Ask Mississippi slaves, ask Montana wobblies, ask Ohio lawn-mowing solid citizens, ask the parents of South Boston. And ask Huey Long, ask Huey Long, ask Huey Long.